Banjo

Also by Frank Walker
JACK
THE NAVVIES ARE COMING

Banjo

FRANK WALKER

Illustrations by David Hughes

London
MICHAEL JOSEPH

First published in Great Britain by Michael Joseph Ltd
52 Bedford Square, London, WC1B 3EF
1977

ISBN O 7181 1593 7

Printed by Hollen Street Press, Slough and
bound by Dorstel Press, Harlow.

Chapter I

(1)

The boys were sitting well back from the tow-path beneath an overhang of elder, the two rods held out over the water like inactive antennae. The floats, one red, one white, sat unmoving on the still surface of the canal and after that frustrating day Paul was ready to believe there was nothing left alive this side of the locks. Not one solitary bite since the first cast at ten that morning and now the September twilight was pulling in and a small breeze was sifting through his knitted cardigan.

Although they were not far from the heart of the city, it took little imagination to make believe they were miles out on the moors around Skipton way. From the cover of the elder—they were hiding there so the fish would not see them—there was no indication they were just two amongst half a million; no smoke, no chimneys, and the multi-storey flats were hidden behind the canal's steep banking. They could not even hear the traffic on the nearby arterial road. They were in a peace of midges and flies which danced and buzzed close to the water and occasionally came under the elder to leave the red bump of a bite on neck or wrist.

Paul scratched at his midge bites and grumbled, "We've had it and I'm hungry. Let's go home."

With a dirty forefinger, Puddin pushed the bridge of his glasses higher up his nose as he always did before embarking on a serious argument and he looked even more like the school swot, which he certainly wasn't. But he was the recognised expert on wildlife and he never gave his considered opinions lightly. He turned to look owlishly at Paul and there was more than a touch of sarcasm in his tone.

"The sun," he said, pointing to the west, "is going down. Now's the time they start to feed. Another half an hour and we'll fill the keep net."

"In that case," Paul asked reasonably, "why have we been here all day?"

Puddin sighed the kind of sigh used by intellectuals when assailed by morons. "Because fish can be as funny as people and you can't tell what they'll do sometimes. We might have caught summat. Three more casts, then."

"And only three," Paul agreed grudgingly.

Lines were reeled, maggots replaced and floats plumped back into the water.

The sun was very low now, its autumn redness reflecting brightly down the length of the canal between the two locks and the midges were doing the water dance in their millions. Puddin adjusted his glasses by holding the right rim with finger and thumb, the sign that he was about to impart information.

"Now, if this was a trout stream we'd be laughing with all these flies and things to make the fish bite. We'd catch enough to open a shop in the market."

He had never cast a fly in pursuit of gamefish but his voracious reading of any book on wildlife or nature had given him a certain amount of authority which no one had ever questioned. Leopards, platypuses, camels, llamas, he knew them all, their feeding habits, mating habits—about which he was eternally questioned—which were tameable and which were not and the only television shows he would admit to watching were *Survival* and kindred programmes. He took hold of the right rim of his spectacles again, preparatory to launching into a lecture on the difference in wet and dry fly fishing when, without warning, a black object sailed from behind them high over the elder to fall with a smack into the middle of the water.

It was an old coal sack, tied at the neck, and it did not sink passively to the bottom like a sack of coal should. It struggled. Not with mad panic as though it contained a

(8)

fierce tom cat but nevertheless there was movement inside as something fought the chilly closing of the water.

Paul sat immobilised with the fascination of horror, knowing he was watching a struggle for life as the sack became saturated and began to sink like a dead, spread-winged bird, knowing whatever was in the sack had seen its last daylight. With a gurgle, a great bubble of air escaped and the sack started to submerge at a faster rate. The movements of the trapped something had never been vigorous and, as Paul watched, they became feebler.

But Puddin, the leader, jumped up and tried to draw the sack to the canal bank with the tapered end of his rod. The tip of the fine cane was little thicker than a match stick, totally ineffective as a boat-hook and he cursed, teetering out to try to use the thicker second section. He dipped it under the sack, bending the supple rod nearly double as he heaved to lever it to the surface. He turned his contorted face to Paul who was still sitting mesmerised.

"Don't sit there, I can't hold the bloody thing all day."

Suddenly reanimated, Paul jumped up and almost danced with helplessness, "What can we do? There's nowt to reach it with."

Puddin strained back on the rod with all the facial expression of the professional martyr. "I can hold it while you get in. Take your strides off, there's no one about."

Paul stopped his jittering and gaped at Puddin. "Go in? Me mam'll murder me if I go home wet through again ..."

He stopped lamely as Puddin contorted his face even more to show the terrific fight he was putting up to save a life and with a guilty look around, Paul unbuckled his belt, dropped his trousers, kicked off his sandals and socks and draped his cardigan on the elder. Puddin groaned with the unbearable strain. Paul hitched his shirt under his armpits, sat on the edge of the bank and carefully lowered his legs into the water. Had he turned around and gone in backwards it would have been easy, but as it was he reached a point where he had to let himself go with a rush and keep his shirt clear, or continue to lower himself with bending elbows and let the shirt unfurl. Momentarily he hung in desperate indecision and he hung a second too

(9)

long. With a gasp and a groan Puddin staggered sideways under his load, thumped Paul in the back with his right knee and launched him at least half the distance to the now fully waterlogged sack. Paul's yell of surprise was cut short when his head went under the cold dark water and he came up spitting, gasping and very close to tears.

"Look at me shirt. Me mam'll kill me."

Apparently Puddin had gained his second wind for he was now easily keeping the sack on the surface. He said scathingly, "Never mind your shirt, you can dry it at our house. Fetch the sack."

Miserably Paul waded with ballooning shirt to retrieve the sack and carry it high, clear of the water to the bank. Puddin dropped his rod, took the streaming bag, cut the binding with his penknife and looked inside.

Paul was not having much success at climbing out of the water, the muddy bottom sucked at his feet and stopped him making a good jump. He stood shivering, with his hands up on the coping. "Help us then!"

Puddin was bent over the sack and was lifting things from it. He did not seem to hear Paul and muttered, "Poor little sods."

Paul was of the opinion that *he* was the poor little sod with his mother to face when he got home and, with tears standing on his lower lids, he shouted, "Help me out!"

Absently Puddin half turned, still crouched, took Paul's hand and hoisted him to the bank. Without a glance at his wet friend he switched back to emptying the sack. As the shivering Paul hopped into his trousers and saw what he had rescued he too became absorbed, forgetting his dripping shirt and the mother who was waiting at home to kill him.

On top of the sack now lay six inert pups, tri-coloured black, white and grey but of uncertain breed.

"Are they all dead?" Paul asked through the chatters of his teeth.

Puddin was pressing the chests of two of them, trying artificial respiration and he grunted, "Don't know, but don't stand there gawpin'. See if you can pump any of 'em dry."

(10)

When he had pulled on his cardigan Paul knelt beside him, placed a hand gently on two of the small chests and began rhythmically to push. Puddin abandoned his two and reached over Paul's arms for the last pair.

"Not much chance of savin' any of 'em but they say you've never to give up hope with a drownin' case," he said as he worked. "I read about one bloke a doctor brought round when everyone else thought he'd been dead twenty minutes. Just keep goin'."

With steady pressure Paul worked on his charges and started the tiny streams of water trickling from their mouths. He increased the pressure slightly, putting as much weight as he dared on the miniature rib cages. After three minutes he yelled, "Hey up, then. One of 'em's coming round."

The dog pup under his left hand coughed weakly, snuffled and half opened its eyes. The one his right hand was working on was showing no more signs of life than the other five so he left it to concentrate on the survivor. The dribble of water kept running from the pup's mouth until it coughed a second time and then it was sick. The vomit was mostly water and after a series of retches it lay tiny, defenceless and panting on the coarse wet sacking.

Puddin's eyes glinted behind the thick lenses. He moved round to squat facing Paul, looking into the bewildered eyes of the pup and stroking its head.

"You're lucky mate," he said. "Your brothers and sisters have all had it."

Now that the urgency of the rescue and resuscitation was over Paul was starting to be aware of the cold again. He shuddered and hugged himself. "Well, we can't stop here, I'll get pneumonia ... and what are we going to do with the pup?"

Puddin picked up the bedraggled scrap of life and held it on his lap. His mother would have known he was machinating by the gleam behind the spectacles; she often said she could see the cogs turning in his head, and they were indeed turning at that moment.

He said hesitantly, "You know we can't keep it at our flat."

Puddin lived on the top floor of a ten-storey block and the hard and fast rules of those unnatural habitats is no animals under any circumstances. The inference behind the words was not lost on Paul.

He said quickly, "Well you know my mam won't let me keep it."

The object under discussion stirred on Puddin's lap, raising its head to look out at a world which up to then had not overwhelmed it with kindness and Puddin touched the wet ears. "Looks as though we might as well have left you in the canal ... Banjo."

Paul frowned. "Banjo?"

Puddin's finger traced an almost circular white patch on the small rump and then along a light grey streak from rump to wither. "Look, just like a banjo in them old-fashioned jazz bands they put on the telly."

Paul looked and grinned. "Yeh! Banjo! That's good. I'll bet there isn't another dog in Leeds called Banjo."

Puddin nodded soberly, "In the world! And soon there won't even be him."

Paul had many friends. He had many friends because he was blessed with a truly kind heart and thoughtful consideration for others. His nature was not something that had been shaped on the anvil of life, there had not been time for that in his eleven years. He had inherited a great capacity for love from his dreamy father who floated through his days in an enviable euphoria, seeing only the good in people and possessing an inexhaustible supply of excuses for the mean and miserable deeds perpetrated by his fellow man. Paul had also, to a lesser degree, inherited a little of the sharpness of character his mother had been obliged to develop in order to protect her philanthropic husband against those who from time to time tried to take advantage of him. But Paul was basically his father's son and although he often saw through the schemings of Puddin and others, he did not often have the heart to put the damper on and refuse them their little triumphs.

In this instance it was all too plain why Puddin was wearing the doleful expression and Paul said with a frown, "You *know* my ma won't let me keep him. Not after Zip and Jet."

(12)

On one of their expeditions Puddin had extricated a pigeon from a tangle of rusty wire, had named it Jet, declared it would become a world champion racer if only they had a home for it to home into. Because of the rule of the multi-storey flats, Jet was put in the care of Paul who rushed home to his semi-detached Corporation house in order to get his father's permission to become a pigeon fancier before his mother arrived home from a regular Saturday afternoon shopping foray.

Denis Holmes had been as delighted as his son, and they had spent the remainder of the afternoon watching Jet flutter about the living room. But disaster had entered with Madge Holmes. Parcel-laden and weary, she had flung open the door, startling Jet, who had been perched on the picture rail, into madly flapping around the room at head height. Madge had jumped with fright as the grey bird flashed by an inch from her nose, had uttered a muted shriek and was not amused by the laughter of her husband and son when she dropped her packages all over the floor. They were on the verge of calming her down with profuse apologies when her eye lighted on the spot immediately below where Jet had been perched, the spot where his droppings had fouled the recently hung wallpaper, and their cause was lost. Reopening the door she had shooed and howled at the befuddled Jet until she had succeeded in stampeding him into the open air, out where he belonged.

The episode of Zip the grass snake had had a much more painful ending for Paul. On opening its box one morning, he found it had escaped, terrifying his mother who dared not sit down for days in case it materialised from behind a curtain and slid into her clothing. Paul had had his ears clattered and Madge had taken to wearing trousers instead of skirts regardless of Denis's comforting, "But Madge, love, it's a snake not a mouse."

With each stinging clout on the head Madge had chanted, "No—more—livestock—in—this—house—or —I'll—kill—you."

By the time Paul and Puddin reached the main road it was

quite dark and they trudged along under the yellow lights with the destiny of Banjo still unsettled. Puddin, of course, was carrying the pup and Paul both fishing baskets and rods. They had wrapped Banjo in an emptied maggot bag and nestled him inside Puddin's windcheater from where he was popping up his head with a seeming interest in the surroundings

Puddin touched the damp nose. "I think you're probably very intelligent. In fact, I shouldn't wonder if you're not already house-trained and wouldn't cause anyone any trouble at all if they took you home. I know I'd take you if we didn't live in a flat ... even if it would mean an argument with my old lady."

Paul humped the straps of the baskets further up on his shoulder. "*Your* old lady isn't as houseproud as mine, is she?"

"True," Puddin nodded, "but your old man'll do owt for you. He'd talk her round. If I had your dad I'd see to it he cancelled the old lady out every time."

"No," said Paul.

"Okay, we might as well walk, then, and hand him in at the R.S.P.C.A. on the way. Here, you carry him a bit, I'll carry the tackle."

Paul readily put down the baskets and exchanged the rods for Banjo. He made a sort of bag with one side of his cardigan and Banjo, still wrapped in the damp maggot bag, sat on his arm looking up into his face as though asking whom he belonged to. They started walking again down Kirkstall Road to the R.S.P.C.A. and Paul had eyes only for Banjo. Every time a car roared by, the small head came up from the folds of wool to investigate the noise and Paul said, "I think you're right. He is intelligent."

"Course, I'm right," Puddin grunted, "but what does it matter where he's goin'."

The quick walk was warming Paul's chilled body and through his wet shirt he could feel the heat coming from the little pup. Every time Banjo moved inside the cardigan or put up his head to look about, it gave Paul a tremendous thrill and by the time they were passing under the viaduct and getting close to the R.S.P.C.A. the

(14)

inquiring brown eyes and dark grey face were taking the first tentative hold of his heart strings. It seemed he had not had hold of Banjo very long when they were turning off Kirkstall Road and passing the television studios and on to Burley Road where the R.S.P.C.A. had their new quarters.

Puddin said, "He might be all right in there, you never know."

Paul said, "Course he'll be all right. Why shouldn't he be? They look after 'em in the R.S.P.C.A., that's what the place is for."

Puddin said, "Oh aye, for the week."

"A week?"

Puddin sighed, "Don't tell me you don't know. They keep 'em a week to see if anyone wants 'em but if nobody does ... kaput!"

Banjo snuggled in closer to Paul's chest as Paul snorted, "Don't talk daft. They wouldn't kill a pup."

Puddin hefted both rods in his left hand and repositioned his spectacles with the finger and thumb of his right, "They don't *kill* 'em, they put 'em down. It's painless. And if they didn't, they'd need a place as big as the Empire State Building to keep 'em all in and that wouldn't be big enough. They get hundreds in every week—not to mention cats and other things. Anyway, there's nowt we can do about it, is there?"

"No," Paul said flatly. They walked on.

It was quieter up on Burley Road although they could still hear the cars down on busy Kirkstall Road but they made distant sounds, nothing to perk up the interest of Banjo and shortly, by the even movements of the small chest, Paul knew he was asleep. He tried to glide more than walk, taking long strides with flexed knees and Puddin asked, "What's up, do you want to go to the toilet?"

"Ssshh, he's asleep, I think," Paul stage whispered.

"Good," Puddin whispered back, "it'll be best if he is, then he won't know we've abandoned him when we hand him in."

Paul frowned. "We're *not* abandoning him. We've saved his life haven't we?"

(15)

Puddin's muttered answer was so soft Paul nearly missed it, "We might as well have left him in the canal for all the good we've done."

Paul had not at any time offered or promised to take Banjo home, he had said the opposite, that he would not take him home, but Puddin's silent insinuations were getting through to him and making him feel uncomfortably guilty. The guilt became stronger and more distasteful as they closed in on the R.S.P.C.A. In a few minutes he would hand Banjo over to a uniformed official who would take him along to the impersonal place where all the other unwanted pups were kept until their week was up. One week of grace in which to make someone like you enough to take you home or you got the chop. Unwanted. Discarded. Thrown into the canal and saved for the hypodermic syringe. One of Paul's teachers had said the most helpless thing on earth is a human baby but what could be more helpless or less able to take a hand in its own fate than this warm, snuggling Banjo lying sleeping on his arm under his cardigan. He coughed and swallowed as they turned from Burley Road into Cavendish Street. Here the lights were fewer and along the street Paul knew one of the dark patches was the R.S.P.C.A. building.

As they cleared the last of the other buildings he saw there was a light on in one of the upstairs rooms and he wondered if that was where the pups were put painlessly to sleep.

Puddin said, gruffly, "Come on, let's hurry up, I want to get home."

Paul's leather soles slapped on the concrete ramp, the ramp the vans backed down to take away the animal corpses, and they stopped at the first door. With his nose close up, Puddin read the white words on the sign, *"Entrance for Boarders Only"*.

Paul's forearm muscles flexed under Banjo. "No good *us* knockin' at that one."

They moved along the face of the building to the main glass doors with the foyer inside and again Puddin read slowly by the light thrown from the street lamp:

(16)

"Royal Society for the Prevention of Cruelty to Animals. Animal Shelter. Open Monday to Saturday 9am to 5pm Closed Sunday. New Homes Wanted for Dogs and Kittens 9am to 4.30pm daily. Clinic Monday Wednesday and Friday 2pm to 3.30pm."

He read the last item through before repeating it aloud and when he did he laid heavy emphasis on every word, *"Destructions 9am to 4pm daily."*

Destructions. As though Banjo was an old three-piece suite or something. Paul looked through the glass doors into the dark foyer and he whispered, as though he was afraid someone upstairs would hear and come to let them in. "Seein' as it's closed, I'll take a chance and take him home till tomorrow," and he hurried away up the steps leaving Puddin to reshoulder the baskets. Puddin followed with a very satisfied gleam behind the glasses.

Paul waited for him under the first street light, "What about the dead 'uns?"

Puddin put down the baskets again and rummaged in his pockets. With a small piece of pencil he wrote on a page of a pocket diary, 'Five dead pups in sack on canal bank near brewery. Under elder bush.' He ran back to the door, pushed the note through the letter box, bounded up the steps and they were off again, walking quickly to the bus stop in the city centre.

They waited for the 77 in the Headrow outside the Town Hall and they waited in silence, Paul's mind occupied with making up some kind of a tale to get round his mother's objections to giving Banjo board and lodgings for the night, and Puddin very circumspectly holding his tongue and trying to stay in the background. After an age the bus ground up, shuddered to a halt and Paul was on the platform before the doors were fully open. Puddin struggled on with the baskets and rods. The conductor/driver looked at Paul and suspiciously at the lump under his cardigan and raised his eyebrows. Paul put a five-penny piece on the ticket machine, "Torre Road, please ... and how much for the dog?"

The conductor/driver craned to look over the machine, "What dog?"

Paul pulled back the cardigan and Banjo's inquisitive

(17)

head popped up to look wide-eyed at the conductor, who replied straight faced, "We charge for dogs, not mice. Go on."

On the back seat Paul took Banjo out, unwrapped the maggot bag and sat the pup on his knee. Puddin stacked the baskets in the luggage space near the centre door and flopped down wearing his serious look.

"We ought to find out how old he is."

Paul was smilingly having a finger licked. "Why?"

Puddin raised finger and thumb to his glasses. "So's you'll know what to feed him on tonight. A pup's diet is important you know, they can choke just like babies if you give 'em the wrong stuff, an' if he hasn't been weaned, it'll have to be milk."

Paul held up Banjo and perched him on the top of the backrest of the vacant seat in front. "Well, how old do you *think* he is?"

The bus groaned, rumbled and juddered away up the Headrow, the sudden violent vibration scaring Banjo into struggling to be released. Paul sat him on his knee again and said soothingly, "Don't be fright. Never fear when Paul Holmes is here."

Puddin pulled the pup's lips away from the teeth and studied the molars intently. "Well, I reckon he's weaned so he's over six weeks. It'll be all right to give him summat mashed up—taties with a bit of meat and a drop o'milk."

Paul was always awed by Puddin's confidence in his own knowledge. He asked, "How do you tell their age by lookin' at their teeth?"

Puddin shrugged. "You just know, that's all. Practice."

Paul was intrigued. "But how—   "

"And don't give him cold milk from the fridge, warm it up to blood heat—you know what that is?"

"Er ..."

"Ninety-eight point four or till it's the same as your elbow."

All the way down Eastgate, round the big loop of Quarry Hill, up Burmantofts Street, Puddin lectured on the do's and don'ts for young pups. He talked about minced chicken, eggs beaten in milk, minced steak and

(18)

fillets of haddock from which every hair-like bone was to be removed before it was cooked gently in milk or double cream. At that moment there was nothing so important as the correct diet for a pup, the perfectly balanced meals that would build bone and muscle, stamina and strength, and the earlier instruction of 'taties with a bit of meat' was washed from the record. Now there had to be nothing but the best for Banjo.

"But," Paul asked slightly puzzled, "does it make a lot of difference for just one night?"

Puddin's right forefinger pushed up his glasses. "Condemned men get the best of treatment the day before they're hanged so surely a pup can have it, specially when all it's done wrong is to get born."

Paul could not answer that one, and the bus was turning into Nippet Lane, time to get off.

Puddin crossed the road and set off briskly up Torre Road, taking the view that the sooner Paul got home and made the introductions the better, but Paul, quite naturally, was not as eager. He still had not made up a convincing yarn to sway his mother, whom he expected would pick up Banjo and hurl him with all her indignant strength into the far distance. He hurried to catch up.

"What am I goin' to say?"

"What's wrong with the truth?"

Paul's mind had been ranging among the fantasies for some heartbreaking story to sway his unsympathetic parent, not that he had told more lies than any other eleven-year-old, but now he thought about it the true story was rather a good one and she would not do more than clip his ear for getting his shirt wet.

"That's it," he said determinedly, "I'll tell the truth."

They parted at Paul's front door, Puddin putting down the basket and propping the rod carefully against the wall and going back down the path with a 'see you tomorrow.' His pace was even faster than coming up the road. He knew how sharp Mrs. Holmes's tongue could be.

The living-room light was coming through the orange curtains and Paul heard a brief loud burst of the signature tune of *Hawaii Five O*. His father was watching the

(19)

television. He went quietly round to the back to find the kitchen in darkness and, whispering encouragement to Banjo to bolster his own sinking confidence, he opened the back door and crept inside. The kitchen clock ticked audibly over the raised voices of the intrepid policemen of Honolulu. Paul tiptoed unerringly between the cooker and the table to pause with his hand on the door knob.

He said into Banjo's ear, "It'll be all right," opened the door and went into the living-room wearing the biggest smile he could muster.

His first feeling was of immense relief. His mother was not in. His father, Dozy Denis as he was unkindly called by more aggressive people, turned with the smile of welcome he always wore, saw Banjo's head poking up from the cardigan and raised his eyebrows. "By hell, lad, you're askin' for it, aren't you?"

"Where's me mam?"

Denis Holmes held out his hand for the pup and answered as he appraised his son's latest adoption, "Still at the bingo. Whose is this?"

"No one's."

Paul told him the story of the rescue with not too much dramatisation and his father heard him out with an occasional nod of the head.

"Well, I suppose I'd have done the same thing meself. And you could hardly just turn him loose just because the R.S.P.C.A. was closed. It'll be all right for one night."

Paul was not convinced. "But what about me mam? You know what she said she'd do to me when Zip escaped."

"But you've still took the chance on fetchin' him home." Denis Holmes put Banjo on the floor and watched as he trotted to stand listening under the television set. He continued, pointing at Banjo, "Your ma's like a lot o' them fellers, her bark's worse than her bite. I'm not sayin' she'll be pleased but she won't have the heart to turn him out in the night, either."

Paul grinned. "I don't care about gettin' me lughole clattered as long as she lets him stay. Don't you think we ought to give him something to eat?"

Denis hauled himself out of the armchair and picked

(20)

Banjo up. "Let's see what there is in the kitchen."

Madge Holmes was one of the last out of the former cinema because she had won a share in the last house. Two other women had screamed 'Bingo' with her but she was eleven pounds fifty pence the richer. She strolled the hundred yards down the street to her gate recounting, drop by drop, the sweat she had lost waiting for the winning number to be called. Her companion sniffed her envy and Madge walked through the open gate wearing a cat-with-the-cream smile on her face and the warm glow of the successful gambler in her breast.

She went to the back door, threw it open, entered her kitchen beaming and saying, "Guess who won toni—"

She stopped, with her mouth open. Her son was at the cooker with his shirt sleeve rolled up and his bent elbow inside a pan. She walked to him amazed, and looked into the pan.

"Milk? What're you doing, trying to give your elbow a nice complexion?"

As Paul had been rehearsing his cheery smile for the last ten minutes it was not altogether spontaneous, and when he said, "We've got a surprise for you in the living-room," the edge very quickly wore from her own jubilation.

"Oh aye—" she answered in a voice that was rapidly acquiring a coat of icicles, "and what have you been up to now? And what the hell are you standing there for with your elbow in that pan o' milk?"

Paul's attempt to make his smile wider made him look ghastly, as though he were in pain and bravely trying to hide it and, if he knew his mother, he was very shortly going to be in that pain. He was still searching for the right words to break the news when he was saved by his father's voice.

"Madge, love, come in here, will you?"

With a withering suspicious look at the milk and then at Paul she went, fearing the worst, in to her husband. Pausing for a moment in the doorway, she pulled it closed behind her and left Paul almost dancing in his anxiety to hear what was going on.

He judged the milk was now at the required temperature, dried his elbow, poured the milk into the ready basin and went to the living-room door. He stopped with his hand on the knob. He could hear his father's voice but on the television a choir of young people were singing the Coca-Cola advertising song and he could not make out what was being said. So he bided his time.

It was not long, but it seemed long to Paul, until his father shouted, "Come on wi' the milk, this pup's dyin' o' thirst."

Paul pushed open the door and walked carefully, eyes fixed on the milk. With his outer vision he could see his mother's eyes fixed on his face but he stared doggedly into the basin as he crossed the room to his father. Had he looked at his mother, he would have read an expression of puzzled love, the love which was always evident even through her scolding and slappings had he looked deep enough, and the amazement that this unaggressive son of hers would risk the promised retribution to give aid to yet another stray animal. Denis Holmes had not had to talk too long to persuade her that Paul had not disobeyed her orders simply to be a little boyish. In his young mind, he had taken a calculated risk in the firm belief that it would be worth a good spanking to see the pup was looked after. Madge Holmes steadfastly kept the smile from her face as Paul, still with eyes averted, dropped to his knees and put the basin under Banjo's nose.

Banjo was thirsty but whoever had thrown him into the canal had let him live long enough to discover how to lap and with braced legs, pricked ears and stiff tail he hung his head in the basin working his small tongue like a piston. Paul very lightly stroked the tips of his fingers down the fuzzy back and forgot his father, his mother, the blaring television. He heard but he did not register his mother's words, "Only for one night, think on."

Chapter 2

(2)

When Banjo woke up, the dawn was filtering through the curtains. He stood up, stretched his hind legs and tried to see over the side of the cardboard box. He knew he was in the strange room to which he had been brought by the boy but he was lonely. He missed the warmth of his brothers and sisters and wondered where they were. But he missed his mother most. She was a big, fond, shaggy crossbreed, always ready to present her offspring with a pendulous breast when they came snuffing at her belly.

Banjo was now thirsty. He didn't know where his mother was but he did know she was not in that box with him and so the first thing to do was to get out. Then he would find her and play with the rest of the litter.

The sides of the box weren't rigid. They gave outwardly as he jumped to hook his paws on them, putting him off balance and tumbling him back into the bottom, but the light was strengthening and coming into the box he could see its dimensions. It was longer one way than the other. After several more attempts to scale the sides where the box was narrow, something in his small mind told him greater speed would lift him higher so he took a run of two feet, which was the length of the box, and threw himself upward. He did well. He hit the top edge with his chest and then it was easy. A mad scrabble with his hind legs, a heave of his body and he fell outside onto the carpet. After giving himself a quick shake he set out on his quest.

He travelled first across the thick pile of lambswool hearth-rug, an almost new off-white lambswool hearth-rug, still new enough to be Madge Holmes's favourite possession. It was no great distance across the rug but the needs of pups are needs that manifest themselves without warning, and untrained pups relieve themselves of these manifestations also without warning. When he went on his way to look behind the settee, the rug was decorated with a damp circle almost in its geometrical centre.

Banjo's mother was not behind the settee, nor was she under the sideboard or in any of the corners. He was baffled. She should be here, she was always here. When he had been put into the sack and carried away, he had known it would not be for long, that he would be brought back to her and even when he had been fighting for his life inside the sinking sack, even through all the frightening terror of the water, he had known for sure that somehow he would get back to her. For she was his mother and she was always there. Banjo stood undecided by the rubber plant and he whimpered. Sometimes when he whimpered, his mother would come to him with her loving tongue that always took away fear and loneliness, but she did not come.

Then Banjo saw the kitchen door which was standing ajar and having another place to search drove the sadness from him. The kitchen window faced east, so it was lighter in there and he could see at once there was no sleeping mother and litter. But there were other things which occupied his mind and stopped him from being unhappy. This room was smaller, the furniture placed much closer together, making the underneaths of tables and chairs more exciting to explore. And there were many smells, some of them so thrilling they brought saliva running into his mouth. But first the search. Again there was no mother waiting for him anywhere. But there were still the smells and they seemed to be coming from everywhere, some of them from above him.

He looked up at the table. It was high, but there were chairs beside it and beside one of the chairs was a small wooden stool of the kind much liked by young children who want to sit with their feet touching the floor like adults. The leap onto the stool was easy but to get up to the chair was harder and he made four attempts, once falling right back to the ground before he succeeded. The table almost defeated him. It seemed to be all space, nothing on which to lever himself upward, but he tried. He tried twice, falling right back to the ground the second time and he had to make the ascent of the chair again. But then he saw the window-sill and that made everything easy. It was a small hop onto the sill and not a very big jump from there to the table top and he was soon finding out where the smells were coming from They were coming from the remains of the food on a supper plate, a plate Paul had nicely forgotten to wash, as instructed by his mother, before going to bed.

The plate held some pieces of hard toast, a fragment of fried egg and a small heap of baked beans. The egg smelled the most interesting so he ate that first, then the beans, the taste of which he was not too sure about but he ate them anyway, and then there was the toast. Paul always left the crusts of toasted bread but Banjo didn't mind them at all, in particular the traces of butter they carried. He treated them as bones, bellying down on the table cloth and holding them in his paws and gnawing away until they were pulped enough to swallow. He enjoyed the initial crunch of his teeth into the crispness and the taste as the butter melted on his tongue, and as the daylight got stronger and getting-up time closer, the table got messier and messier with toast crumbs.

The toast did not last forever but there was a glass container handy full of a white powder. The powder gave off very little smell so Banjo tasted it with his tongue and was very pleased with its sweetness. Because it was powder he lapped at it like milk or water, like a child dabbing a wet finger into sherbet.

The egg, beans and toast, and sugar had not done much for his thirst but on the other side of the plate there was a tumbler with what looked like a drop of milk in the bottom. As a straight line is the shortest way, Banjo walked across the plate and through a small pool of tomato sauce, and as he moved round the glass sniffing at the milk he left an incriminating ring of red paw prints.

There was some milk in the bottom of the glass but the

(27)

glass was tall and Banjo's muzzle short, but he had not come this far to quenching his thirst to be defeated so easily. He thrust his muzzle hard down into the tapering glass and stretched his tongue out at the milk. He could not reach to lap at it. He pressed his muzzle in farther and when he could not reach it that time he knew he never would, so he gave up and lifted his head. But the glass came with it, wedged firmly over his face. He shook his head. The glass stayed where it was. He shook his head again and the glass remained. He struck at the glass with a front paw and that loosened its hold a little so he struck again. The glass landed on the table on its side and Banjo watched it roll away. When it went over the edge and hit the floor with a splintering sound he was unmoved; there were many things yet to be investigated in this kitchen.

He used the original route down to the floor: the sill, to the chair, to the stool, a stretch and a yawn before a quick look round for something else interesting. There was another partly open door and when he put his head in there he knew where most of the nice smells were coming from. He had found the pantry.

Behind the door were three shelves, the bottom one out of his reach, but near to the bottom one was an enamelled potato bin. The enamel was smooth, not giving much purchase for paws to cling to but Banjo was persistent and eventually he scrambled onto the lid. Six inches from his nose was a large bone, and at one end was a fair amount of meat intended to make lamb sandwiches for Denis Holmes's pack-up. The lamb smelled very good and it was not much more than a short hop, even for Banjo, from the bin to the deep shelf. The bone, on a platter, was about as long as he was and as he tested the meat with a lick he discovered the collected juices on the bottom of the plate. These were very good and he butted the bone out of the way to get at them until the plate was clean; then, there being plenty of room on the shelf, he bellied down again and started on the meat.

He heard the noises, but only vaguely because he had never tasted anything so delicious as that meat. He could

(28)

only gnaw at it and tear off small pieces but the flavour held him riveted.

The Holmes family came downstairs together, Denis to go to work, Madge to make up his lunch and see him off and Paul, for once not a laggard, to see Banjo.

Paul looked up dismayed from the cardboard box, "He's gone."

"He can't have gone far," Denis smiled.

"He'll go far when I catch him," shouted Madge from the kitchen. "Just come and look at this mess."

Denis murmured, "Oh, crikey," as they went to see.

Denis looked round as Paul helpfully picked up the broken glass. "Just a few crumbs, love, we'll clean it up," and started to fold up the table cloth.

"Just a few crumbs?" Madge said in a voice they both well knew. "Just a few crumbs? What about the glass and have you noticed the sugar bowl! Where is that bloody dog?"

Denis flapped the table cloth outside the kitchen door and said gently, "Hardly a dog, love, it's only a baby," and Paul added, rather indiscreetly at that time, "That's all he is, Mam, he'll learn."

"Not here, he won't," said his mother very definitely. "One night you said and one night it is. You get straight home from school and take it down to the R.S.P.C.A. D'y'hear?"

Paul was brushing the fragments of glass into a dustpan and he looked up, "But, Mam—"

"Never mind but Mam. I've told you. Where is that bloody little thing, anyway? It can't have got out."

She found that bloody little thing when she went into the pantry for the bread and meat, and any hope Paul might have had of coercing his father to intercede on Banjo's behalf were blown sky high with the near shriek with which she announced her discovery. Denis shook his head in hopelessness and Paul kept his mouth shut.

Banjo enjoyed that day. He was tied by a long piece of string to the clothes post in the back garden and allowed to do as he wished as far as the string stretched. There were birds to chase away and twice Madge came out to give him some milk, once with some biscuit and some of the ruined lamb mixed in, and he only remembered his mother three times. He slept often in the warm September sunshine. When he saw Paul coming up the garden path he ran to the end of the string. Paul went into the house and Banjo heard voices, faintly at first, then louder, then after one loud blast from Madge, Paul came out again, untied his string, picked him up and they set off down the path.

They went for a long walk down a busy road, through the scurry of crowded streets and Paul talked all the time in a soft apologetic voice that trembled on the edge of tears. Paul had wanted Puddin to come but Puddin had other business.

The city was a place of a million interests to Banjo. The shouts of the newspaper sellers, roar of engines, honking of horns, the brightly lit shop windows were all wonders to be stared at as they passed, even if he didn't understand them. And then they were out of the shopping centre and back onto the quieter roads and streets and Paul stopped talking to him.

Eventually they went down some steps and into a building where a young woman was sitting behind a desk just inside the doorway. There was a queue of three and Paul took his place at the end. The one being attended to was a girl of about fourteen with a very old, very fat dog who was having trouble with his breathing. Another young girl came from somewhere inside the building, gently took the lead of the old, fat dog from its mistress and slowly led it down a long, dim corridor. The girl who had brought the dog burst into tears and ran out into the street sobbing loudly. Paul swallowed and coughed. The second customer was an old lady wanting to buy a kitten and when she left she was happily cradling her new infant for which she had paid fifty pence.

The young woman behind the desk looked at Paul, "Yes?"

Paul gulped and spoke all in a rush. "We got this pup out o' the canal last night, me an' Puddin. There was five more but they were dead so I took this one home but me mam won't let me keep it."

(30)

The young woman nodded sympathetically. "I see. Thanks for the note you left. We collected the others. Do you want us to try to find a home for him?"

Paul nodded and held Banjo out to her.

"I'll take care of him," said a voice from behind and when Paul looked round it was the girl who had taken the old dog away.

"Now then," she said to Banjo as she took him from Paul, "you're a nice little lad, aren't you?"

Paul watched her go down the same dim corridor as she had with the old dog and he turned to the girl at the desk, "What'll you do with him?"

Her smile was bright and reassuring. "Put him in the kennels till someone wants him. Don't worry, he'll be all right."

Paul hesitated, not liking to seem distrustful, but he had to ask. "But what if they don't? I mean, if no one likes him?"

The girl shrugged slightly. "We'll keep him a week, that should be plenty of time."

"But what—"

She wagged a finger at him like a schoolteacher. "Now don't you worry about that. Whatever happens, he won't be ill-treated, we do whatever's kindest."

Whatever's kindest. Puddin had told him what that meant. He said "Thanks" very quietly and left the building quickly.

Along the left-hand side of the corridor were doors, but Banjo didn't notice them, he was busy trying to lick the chin of the girl who was carrying him. Unattached to any one person in particular, he took a liking to anyone who showed him kindness and his instinct told him this girl would look after him.

She stopped to open one of the doors and then they were looking into a much shorter corridor, a narrow corridor with a row of wire mesh doors closely spaced on either side, and barking started as soon as she stepped inside. In the first cage-like kennel was an Alsatian as vicious as the reputation given wrongly to the breed. It leaped at its door, alternately barking, snarling and growling at the girl and

(31)

Banjo whom it seemed to hate on sight. Then there was a long stringy mongrel whose bark was of sheer pleasure, a happy dog down on its luck. Next to the mongrel was a Jack Russell yapping incessantly as it raced with its characteristic quickness to and fro from the back of the kennel to the door. Then there was another mongrel, black and shaggy and with bright eyes, and as soon as it saw the girl it sat up and begged appealingly.

The girl opened the last of the kennels and put Banjo inside. He stood looking up from the concrete floor, watching her through the mesh as she clanged and bolted the door. When she turned and went away Banjo ran to the door, pressing his face to the wire as he tried to look obliquely along the corridor to keep her in sight. He heard the door through which he had been brought slam shut and it was as if someone had turned off a radio. All the barking stopped, the dogs waiting in silence for the next visitor.

Banjo looked around his kennel. There was not much to look at, just the sides and wire door and two bowls, one empty and the other full of water. So he had a drink. He paced around the sides of the kennel a few times but quickly grew bored with that. He lay down and went to sleep.

The barking of the other dogs woke him. A man with a deep, gruff voice was opening some of the kennel doors and the dogs were running past Banjo through a door and out into a yard. The man unbolted Banjo's door, held it wide saying, "Come on, then, lad, go an' have a run."

Banjo didn't understand the words, he simply followed the other dogs. There were six: the Alsatian was missing and Banjo never saw that one again. But he enjoyed it in the high walled yard. In a pack they chased about, getting rid of the energy they had no means of using in the kennels, playing at fighting, the bigger ones bowling over the Jack Russell who didn't seem to mind acting as the hare all the time. On his short legs he bounded about, turning like lightning and sending the less agile ones crashing into the wall or rolling in a heap as they tried to copy his quick change of direction. Banjo tried to get into

(32)

the game but he was the youngest and, except for the Jack Russell, the smallest and he was always at the tail end of the pack. But it was great fun and he was tired out when the man with the gruff voice came again to take them in.

It was not fun in the kennel. There was nothing at all to do except eat the food the nice girl brought and have drinks of water that were not really needed but taken simply for something to do. Probably because of this, the breaks in the yard were appreciated out of all proportion, the dogs setting up a louder than ever racket when the man with the gruff voice came into the kennel corridor.

Banjo had no conception of time. Had he not been in the animal shelter, his only means of gauging the passage of the hours would have been day changing to night and the growing hunger in his belly. Time had no meaning for him. The instant he got out in the yard the long periods of boredom were as far away from his mind as if they had never happened. In the shelter, his kennel was lit with an infra-red heating bulb and when he went into the yard it was always daylight and so to him, if he had known about the length of a day, it may have seemed that all time was within the same day.

But the time *was* passing and at nearly every exercise period there would be an old face gone and a new one to take its place.

The other good thing was the visitors, the people who came to the kennels unexpectedly, who walked slowly from door to door, the people who wanted a nice little pet or a big dog to guard the shop. Sometimes they would take a fancy to some lucky dog and he would go off to his new home, straining at the lead to be out in the street, yelping for joy with a furiously wagging tail.

But the days passed and Banjo stayed because except in the eyes of his rescuers he was not really much to look at. He had the appeal of all pups and young animals but a knowledgeable dog person would see his head was too round, his spine too short, his legs too long and his colouring, as noticed by Puddin, was like no other dog's. He was an ugly duckling who would never change into a beautiful swan.

He was always alert with his tail wagging whenever anyone came to look through his door and when a little girl put a finger through the mesh he licked it happily. The little girl's mother snatched her daughter's hand away and said sharply, "What have I told you about that. You can't tell whether they're nasty or not."

Banjo put his short muzzle up to the mesh and the little girl dutifully said, "Gerraway, you smell." And so another opportunity was lost.

One day when the nice girl fed him, she fondled his head and sighed, "Poor little feller, no one wants you. I'd take you home myself but there just isn't room."

She left Banjo with his head happily in his feeding bowl, blissfully unaware of the shortening time and what the seventh day would mean to him.

There came the time when there had been a complete population change in Banjo's corridor, apart from Banjo. He was the only one left of those he had played with on his first exercise period and by now his young mind had forgotten any other existence but the routine of the kennels, the exercise and the feeding and, knowing nothing else, he was happy in a way. He liked to see the visitors but didn't expect anyone to take him away because he had never experienced walking and chasing in parks and fields like his companions had, and he did not bark with them in their appeals for release from confinement.

His day revolved round emptying his feeding bowl, romping in the yard and receiving a little affection from the nice girl. She didn't have much time to fondle him, just a minute or two as she put out his food, but to Banjo it was worth waiting all day for. Down through the centuries since the first wolf was tamed by man into some kind of obeisance and domestication, the canine species had become more and more dependent on man and now an implacable instinct drives a dog to attach itself to a human. As Banjo's week wore on, he looked forward more and more to the visits of the girl and unconsciously started to claim her as his own. The girl knew the ways of dogs and, recognising this, had to swallow hard when leaving him to carry on with her duties. She knew what Banjo did

(34)

not, that his life-span was ticking towards its end, and because he didn't know this his pleasure in her visits, the running in the yard and the feeding times was not lessened.

In the mid-morning of the seventh day, the other dogs started to bark when the door from the outer corridor opened, but it was not another prospective dog owner, it was Banjo's nice girl and she turned to say to someone out in the corridor, "He's in here, last one on the left."

There was a rush of feet and Paul and Puddin were pushing their fingers through the mesh for Banjo to lick.

Paul said excitedly, "We did it, Banjo, me an' me dad talked me mam into letting us have you."

Puddin observed, "Stinks a bit in here. You'll have to bath him when you get home."

Although Banjo did not connect Paul with freedom and getting out of the kennels, he did remember him and his tongue licked at Paul's fingers a little quicker than it might have done at a total stranger.

Paul got up from his knees. "You stay with him while I go an' see about takin' him home."

He went out to the foyer and waited impatiently in a queue of four. When he got to the counter he said quickly, "It's him all right. When can we take him?"

The girl behind the desk looked up quizzically. "You know there's a charge of two pounds?"

Paul hesitated. "But I brought him in an' it's only 'cos me mam wouldn't let me keep him at first, but now she will."

"It's R.S.P.C.A. rules, and we *have* kept him for a week."

Paul didn't have two pounds and he knew this was the seventh day. Both his mother and father were at work and there was no one he could go to for the money.

"But I can't get it till tomorrow."

She smiled. "Tomorrow will be all right."

"But he's been in a week now and you know what you do with 'em after that."

The girl shook her head. "Not when somebody wants him. You can fill the form in now if you like, if it'll make you feel any better, then he'll be yours to come and collect."

(35)

"Well, me mam might not let me have any more time off school. It might be after four before I get here. You won't …?"

She shook her head and smiled again. "No, we won't. We're here to find homes for them, not to put them down. That's only the last resort. He'll be here waiting for you."

Paul filled in a form promising that Banjo would never be anything other than a pet. The form warned that if Paul ever ill-treated the dog the R.S.P.C.A. reserved the right to take him away.

Paul and Puddin stayed on their knees with Banjo for more than an hour until Puddin said *he* had not been given permission to take the day off school and he had to go in that afternoon to get a mark and hoped his father wouldn't notice when he took his report home.

At twenty past four on the following day, the day when Banjo's corpse should have been loaded into the van for incineration, a breathless, red-faced, bright-eyed Paul came to take him home.

The smiling girl behind the counter laughed. "I don't think we need fear what kind of treatment he's going to get from you, young man. Go with the kennel maid and she'll get him out for you."

When the kennel maid, Banjo's girl, put him into Paul's arms he was all licking tongue and wagging tail.

Back at the reception desk, the girl behind the desk said, "Don't forget his licence and to put his name and address on his collar or he'll finish up back in here if he ever gets lost. And how about a lead?"

Paul had fifty-two pence in his pocket, mostly for his bus fare, and although a thin leather lead and collar would cost fifty, he had to have the proper equipment for *his* dog, and they could walk home.

With Banjo dragging like an eager bloodhound on his new lead, they were off at a trot through the doors and into the street, Paul saying to the girls, over his shoulder, "He can't half pull for his size."

Pull Banjo could, full as he was of energy and joy at being able to see more than a few yards again and the two girls laughed as they heard Paul's shouts from the street,

"Stop it. Take it easy. Steady, Banjo, steady, it's all right now."

It was definitely all right now as far as Banjo was concerned. There was space above him, space all around him and an infinity of ground to run on. The desire of all dogs, denied him during the past week, the yearning to run and explore and play, awoke with a bang and he charged up the short hill to Burley Road towing a protesting Paul. Paul was strong enough to have dug in his heels and stopped him but he was afraid of breaking Banjo's neck so he tried to get his pup to see reason with every manner of plea. But Banjo wasn't having any.

His forward progress was not a smooth gallop. There were shop doorways to dive in and out of, lamp posts to sniff quickly at in passing and a pillar-box to run around. He ran round the pillar-box too quickly for Paul and they finished up with Banjo between his feet and the lead in a tangle. Paul doubted the wisdom of not carrying Banjo and going home on the bus. But by the time they reached the Headrow, Banjo was slowing down and when they walked down Eastgate he was docilely walking at Paul's side panting like a marathon runner.

Paul said, "Took the steam out of yourself, haven't you?" but he said it too soon. As they were passing under the entrance arch of Quarry Hill Flats, Banjo got his steam back. He saw another dog and wanted to play, nearly catching Paul napping with a loose hold on the lead but Paul managed to tighten his grip

"Stop it, you little—"

They were off again, running after the playful mongrel. They were heading in the right direction and this time Banjo tired out quickly. When he stopped chasing, the mongrel scratched at its back and then lay down on the pavement. It's no good running by yourself. Paul and Banjo went the rest of the way fairly sedately.

Having given in to her husband and son on the issue of dog-owning, Madge Holmes opened her heart to Banjo. Gas heating had recently been installed, leaving the coal house in disuse. It had a grate in the outside wall for coal

(37)

deliveries and an interior door opening into the kitchen. The previous evening, when the decision to let Paul have Banjo had been made, she had scrubbed out the coal house and enlisted her husband's help in painting the walls with emulsion. Now the floor was covered with an old piece of carpet and she had found two old deep pie plates for feeding dishes. The old coal house made a very good, dry and airy kennel.

The weariness left Paul as he walked Banjo up the garden path and round to the kitchen door—the door Madge insisted Banjo must always use—and when they burst into the house he was full of the joy of his new possession.

"They kept him for us, Dad. He's here!"

"Of course they kept him," Denis smiled as Banjo ran in, "they said they would, didn't they?"

"They might have made a mistake or got mixed up or summat."

"Well they didn't," Madge chipped in, "so stop talkin' so gloomy. I expect he'll be ready for a drink."

"Me an' all. We walked home. I'd no bus fare left 'cos I'd to buy him a lead an' collar."

Madge went into the kitchen to look in the oven, and was followed by the inquisitive Banjo.

"Tea won't be long. Wash your hands and face ... and *you* put your head any further in there and you'll get it burned off."

As the Holmeses ate at the kitchen table, Banjo dined from the old pie plates in his kennel on milk and mashed-up tinned dog food. Madge had bought a variety of popular brands to find out which suited him best.

She said, as she ate, "There's one thing. I want him house-trained right quick."

Paul gulped a piece of potato. "How do we do that?"

His mother pointed at him with her fork. "*I* don't know, so you'd better find out. Ask the brain child, Puddin. I don't want to be running round cleaning dirt up after him all the time."

Denis Holmes' expression was pained. "Madge, can we talk about that when we've finished eatin'?"

Banjo had finished his meat and came out into the kitchen to see if there was anything else to eat. He stood beside Denis's chair with his head twisted, looking up with a big, pleading question mark in his eyes and Denis reached down to scruff his ears.

"Hang on a bit and I'll save you some."

"He's *had* his dinner," Madge protested.

"An' Puddin says they haven't to get too fat," said Paul.

Denis looked down at the expectant Banjo and shrugged apologetically. "Sorry, mate, but you've got to keep slimline."

"And another thing"—Madge could always find another thing to say—"I don't want you letting him lick the plates or owt. It's not hygienic. He's to learn to eat off his own plates and that's all."

"Banjo," Denis Holmes said sternly, "life's goin' to be a bit regimental for you, but you'll get used to it in time."

Paul was first to finish and Madge was waiting to push him back into his seat as he started to rise. "Let your dinner go down five minutes. Your food doesn't do you a bit of good, rushing about like you do."

"But, Mam, I want to catch Puddin before he goes out. I mean, you want to know about house trainin' an' that."

"Five minutes, I said."

The endless five minutes passed and Paul clipped on Banjo's lead. As he allowed himself to be dragged outside his mother called after him, as she invariably did, "Don't be late, half past nine, mind."

And as Paul invariably did, he shouted back, "Right, Mam."

Paul could see Puddin's flat over the rooftops a quarter of a mile away and they ran it all with Banjo somehow managing to sniff at the hedges as they tore along. Paul gasped, "I'll be the fittest in the school before I've had you long." Even then his exertions were not ended. The rule of no animals in the flats meant a discreet entry and that meant the stairs, all ten flights of them. He didn't want to risk bumping into any of the animal-haters by using the lift. No one used the stairs. At the third floor, Banjo sat down panting so Paul carried him. At the seventh Paul sat down but Banjo had recovered and roamed restlessly at the end of his lead.

Paul said, "Give us a chance. I gave you one."

Banjo answered by making a small puddle on the floor and Paul was fast on his feet, climbing again. "The caretaker'll do us if he catches you doin' that. Me mam's right, we'll have to get you house-trained in a hurry."

Puddin's father answered the door. He looked over his spectacles at Paul, then at Banjo and grunted, "In the livestock business again, are we? You'd better come in afore someone sees it."

Puddin met them in the hallway. He grinned. "They didn't do him in, then. Good. Fetch him in to see me mam."

Puddin's mam was as enthralled with Banjo as Paul's had been at first. She sniffed. "An' what's your mother got to say about it?"

"She said I could have him."

Puddin's father, Harry Pease, who had also borne the nick-name of Puddin in his youth, adjusted his spectacles and bent to examine Banjo who was sniffing at his slippers. "What the 'ell's it supposed to be, anyroad? A Japanese Rat Hound?"

He had the irksome habit of bellowing at his own jokes and Paul pulled Banjo protectively away from the interesting slippers.

"We won't know," he said loftily, "until he grows up. Will we, Puddin?"

Puddin pushed up the bridge of his glasses with a forefinger. "Well," he said slowly, "I'm fairly sure he's a crossbreed, but just what—"

His lecture was cut short by another bellow of parental laughter when Harry Pease choked, "You're *fairly* sure? Christ, if there isn't all Heinz fifty-seven varieties in that one ... well I don't know!"

Banjo was irresistibly attracted by Mr. Pease's slippers and Paul pulled him back more roughly. "He's not as bad as that. Anyway, he can run!" Paul fired the only shot he could think of in defence.

Mr. Pease preluded another gale of mirth with, "So

could Mill Reef when it won the Derby, but that's not a bloody dog, either."

Mrs. Pease, who had kept her silence longer than was habitual, warned, "Well, don't fetch it here too often. That caretaker's narky enough as it is."

"Nay," Harry said, contenting himself this time with a grin, "it'll allus be good for a laugh."

Paul had stood all the insults on Banjo's behalf he intended. He said to Puddin, "Are you comin' out then, or what. I'm taking him to East End Park for a bit."

"I might as well."

As they closed the door, Mrs. Pease shouted, "Don't be late an' say you lost the dog and was lookin' for it."

Puddin closed the door with a bang. "She can read my mind. She ought to be on the telly. Come on, I'll race you down."

Fifteen minutes later, Banjo was glorying in his first run on green grass with trees and bushes and other dogs to sniff at. Fifteen minutes after that, he was panting in Paul's arms completely worn out after his first day of freedom.

Chapter 3

(3)

Banjo fitted nicely into the slightly altered routine of the Holmes household. It had been made quite plain by Madge that Banjo was Paul's dog and therefore his responsibility and if anyone had to sacrifice anything in the furtherance of his welfare it had to be Paul.

The first thing Paul had to put on the altar was half an hour's bedtime, a privation he would not have minded so much at the end of the day but Banjo had to be taken out in the mornings. Not that Paul begrudged getting up thirty minutes earlier—not too much, anyway.

When Paul came downstairs fastening his shirt, Banjo would be waiting in a nervous ecstasy of joy at the other side of the closed staircase door. His kennel, the old coal house, was built directly under the stairs and no one could ever creep down without being greeted with a wagging tail and an exhibition of how high a pup can jump.

Paul would stretch and yawn, look through the curtains at the state of the weather, drink milk from the bottle—in contradiction of Madge's orders—and spend five minutes trying to get Banjo to bring his own lead from the kennel floor.

After each failure Paul would say sadly, "How am I ever goin' to get you to sit up and beg? Come on."

They would go over a low part of the fence surrounding the playing fields of a huge factory which had all the amenities of a park but which was literally on the doorstep. All it lacked was trees, but football and rugby goalposts made adequate substitutes and Banjo could romp and make his morning toilet in his own good time. He would run like mad after a thrown ball but ignored all Paul's requests to fetch it. Once it stopped rolling, he would stand over it, looking at Paul and waiting for him to come and throw it again.

"Banjo," Paul would say, "I'm only supposed to be half the team. I'm the thrower, you're the catcher." Banjo would wag his tail and look with eyes bright with fun through the grey fringe growing down his face. But he wouldn't fetch the ball.

Over the months, Paul and his dog became inseparable, almost. The only times they were not together was when Paul was at school, in bed—Banjo was not allowed upstairs—or if he went on one of his rare visits to the cinema with Puddin.

When Madge enquired after her son, she would say to Denis, "Where's me an' my shadow, then?"

For Banjo, had he been able to think about it, life was just about ideal. In the periods when Paul was not at home, he would follow Madge or Denis about or spend a couple of hours on the end of the long rope tied to the clothes post, and have the run of the back garden.

Banjo liked Saturdays best and Paul swore he knew when it was Saturday. He was, incredibly, always that little bit brighter and more excited, running backwards and forwards from the breakfast table to the back door as if telling Paul to hurry up with his breakfast and let them get on with the important things in life—like going to Temple Newsam Park in the morning and to the market in the afternoon.

They went to the park on the bus and Banjo's excitement would start to rise when the bus crested the top of Halton Hill, passed the last of the houses and he could see the golf course on the right stretching up to the mansion house and the swathes of grass on the left broken only by the athletics track. As soon as they stepped from the platform, there were trees glorious trees, masses of them, and Banjo would yelp and strain at the lead to be free to run.

Paul never gave him his freedom until they were clear of

the dangerous bus turnaround. They would walk along the path on the west side of the big house, and when the lead was unclipped Banjo would be away, his claws pattering on the old flagstones as he scampered round the corner onto the terrace, the same south-looking terrace from which Henry VIII is said to have taken the air.

Bygone monarchs did not concern Banjo. From the terrace, curving round to the north, was a great sweep of waving grass and the grass did not wave in vain. The young dog was into it, leaping, frolicking, darting to send birds skyward, rolling and generally showing the world what a good place it was to be in. After him ran Paul, shouting streams of orders, none of which Banjo ever took the slightest notice and Paul, not expecting him to, did not mind.

Banjo always made first for the copse of trees at the edge of the park boundary where the ugly, opencast coal site was and, after searching the copse, tore north along the boundary fence, down the hill to where the water was. Paul knew the route and saved himself a lot of running by cutting diagonally across the grass and getting to the sluggish water of the widened stream first.

There were fish in the water which Banjo could not see and ducks on the surface which he could and while he was in the park the ducks knew no peace. He would plunge in, wading in the shallow and swimming in the deep, but always duckwards. He never had a chance of catching one and it is doubtful whether he would have known what to do if he had, but with him it really was the chase that mattered and he never wearied of pursuing the strange, quacking birds.

Actually he did tire, physically, and it was only when he was absolutely fagged out that he would drag himself onto the bank and collapse, panting like a steam engine, too worn out even to shake himself. That was when Paul would put the lead on him again and wait until Banjo had recovered—a process that didn't take too long—and shaken the water from his lengthening coat, before taking him away from the magnet of the water into the woods.

The woods held their own brand of interest: birds,

(47)

squirrels and usually another dog or two to approach with caution and make tentative friends with.

The squirrels provided most fun but no more success than the ducks. Banjo would sight one on the ground and make a mad, crashing rush and the squirrel would easily get to the nearest tree, vanishing around the far side of the bole. By the time Banjo got to the spot where the squirrel had disappeared, a foot or so from the ground, the tree trunk would be squirrelless with the small grey animal looking down from a safe perch thirty feet above him. Banjo would whine, run back and forth and leap at the trunk in his frustration and the squirrel would just sit there looking down, unmoved.

After the woods, there were the football pitches to cross to complete the circuit and get back to the bus stop, and here there were always dogs out for their constitutional. This was where Paul had most trouble catching him and other owners, whose dogs would return when called, shook their heads and offered all kinds of advice on how to make a dog obedient. But Banjo was Paul's first dog and both had much to learn.

When they got off the bus, they didn't go straight home, they had an errand to do first. They had to go to the fish and chip shop for the regular Saturday lunch. Banjo had many favourite places and this was one of them. He would stand beside Paul in the queue in a mouth-watering cloud of gloriously scented steam, his eyes never leaving the man behind the counter, for the man behind the counter never failed to drop a cold chip or two for Banjo whilst he filled Paul's order.

On the few minutes' walk home from the fish shop Banjo was drooling, eager, full of animated impatience and he was forever leaping to get his nose as close as possible to the fragrant newspaper parcel under Paul's arm. Fish and chips are one smell to a human but to a dog they are a tantalising cocktail of scents and he could pick out the haddock from the potato, the batter from the vinegar and even the dripping in which the meal had been fried, and he loved them all, as he loved anything edible.

His early eating pattern had not lasted long. The one

thing Madge had taken charge of was his diet and she had
carefully doled out the advised quantities of dog food for
growing pups. These measured meals had never taken
more than a few minutes for Banjo to demolish and she
had been worried that they had guessed his age wrong and
were giving him insufficient proportions but an old wise
neighbour, who had owned many dogs and therefore
claimed to know all there was to know about them, had
said sagely, "Dog food! None o' mine've ever had any. Give
'im what you have. Anyway, poor little buggers are
entitled to a bit o' Yorkshire puddin' now an' again, aren't
they? After all, they're only human."

So Banjo had been put on, and evidently flourished
under, the same diet as his master. And he seemed to love
it. Tomato, chicken, celery, mushroom or oxtail soup, meat
and veg, casserole, steak pie, stew and dumplings; rice
pudding, apple pie, jam roll and custard, semolina—all
went down with the same relish and speed. He even liked
tea with or without sugar. But best of all he liked Saturday
lunch with its fish and chips in his dish and no frills or
waiting for humans to finish one course so he could get on
with the next.

After Saturday lunch—and after Paul's five minutes'
enforced digestion time—the lead came out again and they
took Paul's pocket money into town to find things to spend
it on. Banjo was as familiar with all the large department
stores as he was with the small out-of-the-way shops which
specialised in selling things designed to delight the heart of
young boys. But most of all Banjo liked the big, crowded,
covered market with its unbelievable variety of smells and
things to look at, things unknown but with which he would
have done anything to become acquainted. Like the lines
of plump pheasants hanging overhead in the game stalls,
the ranks of dressed turkeys and chickens and rabbits, the
cheeses, sides of bacon and pink boiled hams. When Paul
was evaluating some gadget on a novelty stall, Banjo would
sit facing the other way drinking in the aroma of uncooked
skate, plaice and halibut. Had Banjo been able to reason,
he would not have thought highly of Paul's choice of what
money should be spent on. Except one item. Cockles. They

(49)

were Paul's weakness and they always stopped at the small shellfish bar just inside the market entrance where he bought two miniature plates of cockles. He, the gourmet, chewed all the flavour from each one and Banjo, the gourmand, swallowed them whole.

"You'll get guts-ache," Paul once admonished and was overheard by the lady behind the counter who grinned.

"It's whelks he wants, like my poodle. They don't swallow *them* whole."

So whelks replaced cockles for Banjo's afternoon snack and as the lady had said, he didn't swallow them whole but had to put in some jaw work to pulp the rubbery mollusc into a swallowable consistency.

"Gerroutathat," Paul grinned, glad for once to have won an argument with Banjo. Banjo looked up through his fringe and stretched his wide mouth in what surely must have been a grin.

They had two calls to make on Saturday afternoons. One was to a particular stall which, according to Madge, sold the only tomatoes worth eating and the second was to her favourite butcher for the week's meat supply. Banjo would stand passively at the vegetable stall but at the butcher's, which was in the long row of meat purveyors, he was at his best lip-licking attention, eyes switching from salesman to salesman as they came to the scales to weigh the orders. Paul, a regular at the shop, was known as a good spender and so his dog was eligible for reward. Each time the man serving Paul came to the scales with the joint, shin, chops, kidney and the other items on the list he would toss a piece of scrag end or other trimming to Banjo's ready mouth and Banjo was never caught napping, he was always ready for some more.

It was in the queue at the butcher's that Paul picked up a little more dog lore, something Puddin, for all his knowledge, had never mentioned. A very old lady was in front of Paul and she immediately fell for Banjo, turning to pet and stroke him and give him a backhanded compliment.

"Ee, you're a funny lookin' 'un, but you're lovely. What's his name?"

(50)

"Banjo!"

She cackled loud, cracked laughter. "A funny name for a funny dog." Then she bent to stroke Banjo again and said softly, "My Bambi was a little terrier. I wish I'd had him done."

"Done?" Paul enquired politely.

"Aye," she sighed, "injected at the vet's. He got distemper."

Paul had heard of the disease but had never encountered it. "Is it bad?"

"He died."

"Do they all die?"

The old woman shook her head and sighed again, "Not all of 'em, but it can leave 'em with damaged brains an' all sorts. If I could afford another dog I'd have him injected straight away ... poor little sod."

She seemed very close to tears which was embarrassing to Paul who was glad for two reasons when his order was ready. First, to get away from the possible proximity of a weeping female and secondly to get home and tell his father that a visit to a vet was vital. He accepted his change and picked up the plastic carrier bag.

The old woman said, "Think on, you get him done as quick as you can. They pick distemper up in all kinds o' places."

"I will," said Paul, hauling Banjo away from the alluring scent of blood.

It was no dawdling stroll that day, the walk home from town, it was all speed with no stopping for sniffing sessions since the old woman's scanty information on the canine disease had given Paul an urgency which almost amounted to panic, as if at any second he expected Banjo to curl up and expire.

Into the house they rushed, dropping the bag on the kitchen table, and through into the living room where Denis was enjoying a snooze on the settee.

"Dad!" Paul piped in a voice matching his worried frown, and Banjo jumped onto Denis's chest to lick him awake. Startled, Denis opened his eyes and shot up, tumbling Banjo to the floor.

"What's up, then?"

"It's Banjo, we've to take him to the vet's."

Denis squeezed his eyes shut and blinked, he sat forward as Banjo stood upright with his front paws on his knee. The tail, stragglier by the week, was wagging, the eyes under the growing fringe were bright, the tongue, pink and wet, was reaching for his hand and Denis blinked again.

"There seems to be nowt wrong with him."

"Not yet, but a woman at the butcher's said if we don't have him injected, he'll get distemper an' then he'll die."

Denis yawned and stretched. "Put the telly on for the football results. Don't panic about the dog. Maybe you're right, but we'll find out an' if he wants doin' we'll have him done."

"But Dad!"

Paul left his plea unspoken. Kindly and considerate as his father was, hurried he could not be. He would make enquiries and act if necessary. So Paul took his own precautionary measures. He assumed that distemper, like other diseases, was contracted by contact with the disease, and as distemper seemed peculiar to dogs, the best thing was to keep Banjo away from his brothers. On the Sunday morning, instead of a run in the park, they went for a walk in the streets with Paul shooing away any dog which looked like coming within sniffling distance.

Banjo was growing now, the long legs and the short hairy body sprouting visibly and as his belly got further away from the ground his fringe came down to cover more of his eyes. Not that the dark grey curtain had any apparent effect on his vision and some instinct warned Paul to resist his mother's half-joking offers to give Banjo a 'haircut'.

"He'd look lovely," Madge Holmes said thoughtfully, "with his fringe trimmed and waved and a ribbon round his neck."

Paul snorted. "Mam! He's a dog, not a posh woman's poodle. Promise you won't do it when I'm at school."

Madge smiled and bent to look closely at Banjo's fringe. "Who'd be a lovely lad, then."

"Mam!" Paul said with what was very near to a threat in his voice.

(52)

Madge relented her teasing and laughed and Paul was slightly mollified, but as his father had told him on the quiet, you can never tell what women are likely to do.

On the Monday evening when Denis came home from work he shouted, as he accepted Banjo's bouncing greeting, "Is the tea ready, Madge? We've to be at the vet's before seven."

"Ready to put out," she told him, coming from the living room. "Give Paul a shout, he's gone next door."

Paul never needed more than one call at meal times; like his mongrel mate, he was always hungry and whenever Paul's name was called round about that time of day it was always answered in duplicate with Banjo usually appearing first to sit smartly and expectantly at attention in the doorway of his coalhouse-kennel. Madge could never help smiling at Banjo's intent face as he sat with all his senses aimed at the closed door of the cooker.

"How long have they called *you* Paul?" she asked as she lifted out the meal. Banjo answered with a quick wipe of his tongue round his drooling lips.

Paul was excited about going to the vet's, firstly because it was for Banjo's good and also because he had never seen the inside of a vet's surgery and like all boys he looked forward to new experiences.

"Which one are we off to?" he asked his father, spearing a sausage and biting off the end.

"Use your knife and fork properly," his mother chanted automatically, adding sharply, "and you get back in there," to Banjo who had already disposed of his sausage and mash without the aid of cutlery.

"They say Morton's the best. It's a bit of a way, at Meanwood, but if we've got to go we might as well go to the best."

Paul nodded sagely in full agreement, and as he chewed the sausage he smoothed his mash with his knife and then drew a symmetrical grid with the prongs of his fork. Paul was prone to absent-minded meal-time doodling and his mother often made him jump, which she did then, by snapping, "I said use your knife and fork properly, not for making patterns. And *you* get back in that kennel!"

(53)

Banjo had been slyly slinking to Paul's side in the hope he would drop something from his fork—it was not unknown—but he turned, the picture of dejection with head hung low and ears drooping, back to his kennel.

Madge kept her eyes on him all the way and when he proposed to lie in his doorway she pointed at him, "I said, get inside."

Banjo moved his position another two inches further and lay with his head on his paws, keeping his eyes turned away from Madge.

Madge had a thought. "How much do these injections cost, Denis?"

Denis carefully heaped mashed potato on his fork, "Not much."

"*How* much?"

On the basis that a graceful lie is better than an ugly truth Denis said, "About a pound," and filled his mouth.

As Madge poured the tea she sniffed, "It's enough, as well."

They went by bus to Meanwood, Denis showing surprise at the way Banjo took up his station unobtrusively by the window. "He seems to know what's expected of him, Paul."

"Trainin', Dad," Paul said casually. "I allus make him sit in the same place when we go to the park or to town. Puddin was right. He is intelligent."

The vet's surgery was a large stone house standing in its own grounds. They walked in the door marked 'enter' and triggered off a bedlam of barking. Evidently it was the habit of the patients who were killing time in the waiting-room to relieve the monotony by blasting away at any new arrival with full company and chorus. A doleful Bloodhound bayed a deep bass to the hoarse gruff of a Bulldog, the baritone of an Alsatian, the tenor of a Sheltie and the soprano of a Yorkshire Terrier who seemed to find it necessary to imitate a yo-yo at the end of his lead in order to hit top 'C'. These were the principals and they performed to the backing of a close harmony group made up of a quivering–jowled Mastiff, twin Pekingese, a

(54)

three-legged Whippet and a mystery of an animal which reminded Denis of nothing so much as a nervous flue brush.

Several owners glared at Banjo as though they thought he ought to be filling the inside of a tin of dog food instead of setting off their little darlings, and Banjo's bright eyes gleamed out from under his fringe as he greeted one and all with a cheerful grin. Paul and Denis, not sure whether they had broken some unwritten etiquette, stood uncertainly in the doorway by the reception desk whilst ruffled owners tried to quieten their charges to whispered explanations of:

"Bobbles can't stand grey dogs."

"The vet ought to do something, all this barking upsets my little Timmy."

A tall man told his flue brush to shut its bleedin' racket, the elderly owner of the Mastiff put her arms around its great neck and whispered words of comfort into its ear and a very pregnant woman gasped with the effort of bending to scoop up the Yorkie and secrete it somewhere in her clothing as she murmured, "There, it's all right, George." George did not believe her and his muffled yapping continued unabated. Eventually, apart from the protestations of the invisible Yorkie, peace was restored.

A girl in a white coat came from a door marked 'Surgery' followed by a woman carrying a lidded basket. Paul did not know what was in the basket, but Banjo and the rest of the patients did and when the Grand Opera started another performance it was with an extra voice, which was the equivalent of a boy soprano, as Banjo yelped and tried to get at the basketed cat. The woman carrying the basket hurried to the door, pausing before she slammed it, to give the company a withering look. Banjo swaggered triumphantly at the vanquishing of the cat and now that he was accepted by his fellows, peace was gained for the second time.

The girl had gone behind the desk. "Name, please?"

"Holmes."

She opened a drawer of a filing cabinet. "New patient?"

(55)

Denis was unaccustomed to hearing animals referred to as patients. "We've brought the dog."

"Yes. Has he been here before?"

"No."

"Full name and address ... thank you. What's the trouble?"

She took the information and asked them to take a seat.

They sat next to the Bloodhound, a vastly overweight animal, who regarded Banjo with watery eyes and a miserable expression.

Denis chattily asked of its owner, "What's up with him, then?"

The owner's brow furrowed with concern. "I can't stop him putting on weight since I had him castrated."

"Blimey," said Denis with deep sympathy. "I don't wonder he looks fed up."

Banjo was enjoying this outing. The barrel-bodied, huge pawed Bloodhound didn't seem to mind being sniffed at, didn't even seem to notice. His eyes were fixed dismally on nothing in particular as though contemplating his future as a eunuch. But dogs who cannot look you in the eye or return an exploratory sniff are not very interesting and Banjo looked round for some other likely object. He was sitting at Paul's feet and Paul had not yet learned the cardinal rule of dog ownership: never take your eyes off your dog.

Paul was watching the Pekes, one of whom alternated between growling ferociously at the world in general and scratching its belly with a hind paw, and the second who simply stood and panted heavily like an asthmatic old gentleman. Paul also did not obey the second most important rule: keep a tight grip on the lead. The lead was in his hand but his hand rested loosely on his leg and when Banjo sprang across the room Paul was completely taken by surprise.

Banjo had seen something most intriguing. There was a strange movement under the coat of the big-bellied woman sitting across the room. A sort of lump was shifting this way and that on her right side, first moving up a little, then down and then laterally, but never very far and never for long. Whatever it was it was more animated than his neighbour the Bloodhound, and Banjo nipped lightly across to the woman with the intention of putting his head inside the coat for a look. But, being still on the small side and therefore coming up from the ground, he misjudged his target and thrust his head up into the darkness under the woman's skirt, between her open legs. The woman shouted with fright but was unable to jump up due to her condition. The best she could accomplish was to sit stiffly back in her chair with her legs sticking straight out, her whole length at an angle of forty-five degrees. A puzzled Banjo, who had not found the moving object, stuck his head further into the accommodating recently enlarged space under the skirt and the woman screamed hysterically.

Dogs react much more quickly than men and while the humans reacted quite naturally by sitting up with startled looks, the dogs, equally naturally, wanted to join whatever game Banjo was playing. Four of the dogs had inattentive owners, including the flue brush who was the first—and last—of them to push his head up beside Banjo's to see what he could see. Had not the owners then acted with great speed just as the vet burst in from his surgery to investigate the commotion, the pregnant woman would have suffered the indignity of having five dogs, six including her own George of the top 'C', romping about inside her clothing. In concert, the owners sprang forward, a move not entirely collision-free, and the dogs were rounded up to suppressed curses and threats. The vet, Mr. Morton, did not suppress his irascibility. He stood in the doorway, arms akimbo, red faced.

"This is sometimes called the dog house, it's *not* a bloody mad house. Will you keep those animals under control. I'm trying to examine a dog in here."

He stumped back into the surgery and slammed the door. Every human eye was turned balefully on Banjo, every canine tongue hung pinkly as the dogs panted away the excitement of the fore-shortened frolic.

Paul bent to whisper savagely, "Will you behave yourself, you're showin' us up."

(57)

Banjo looked up through the fringe and grinned. Denis said softly, "If you'd been holdin' him right he wouldn't have got away."

The angular lady with the Pekes sniffed loudly, "*Some* people aren't fit to have a dog. Come on, Bobbles, that's a love." Bobbles the panting Peke walked stumpily from under her chair to be lifted onto his mum's knee. The angular lady smirked and stroked his mane.

The owner of the flue brush leant forward to peer under the seat of the Peke owner and asked loudly, "'ave yer gorra bit o' rag in yer 'andbag, missus."

The angular lady looked imperiously down her nose at this uncouth request. "Certainly not—why?"

"'cos your dog's just pissed under yer seat an' ah don't want mine gerrin any more ailments than 'e's got already."

If the angular lady's blood was not cobalt in colour, she was certain it was at least of a Mediterranean hue—as was that of her Pekes—and she turned all the might of a well-practised haughty glare on the owner of the flue brush, a look that had shrunk many a timid daily help, but she directed it now on a fellow who was delighted to cross swords with anyone 'posh'.

"What's up then, dun't your dogs piss, or what?" The outraged face of the lady was saved by the call of, "Next patient, please!" She got up, glared again at her antagonist and marched with banners flying and a Peke under each arm into the surgery.

Paul whispered to his father, "They're not right matey in here, are they?"

Paul and Denis were last in the queue. Mr. Morton said, "Put him on the table and hold his head," as he filled the syringe. A few seconds later Banjo was safe from distemper, as well as several other diseases Paul hadn't heard of.

Mr. Morton said, "That'll be five-fifty for this inoculation and the second one which he must have in a fortnight's time. In twelve months' time bring him back for the booster. The nurse'll give you a vaccination certificate on your way out. Always bring it with you."

The young nurse had the blue booklet ready bearing Banjo's name and address, the batch number of the serum used and at the place marked 'Breed' she had written 'Cross'.

Paul read the card with Denis and asked the girl, "What is he a cross of, do you know?"

The girl laughed. "It's impossible to say. If it wasn't for his tail I'd be inclined to say mostly Old English Sheepdog, judging by his fringe and the shape of his head, but he could be anything. Don't worry about it, it doesn't matter as long as you like him. *He* doesn't know he's not a pedigree, do you, Banjo?"

Banjo wagged his tail and grinned up at the girl with the nice voice.

There was a small worry nagging Paul as they waited at the bus stop—the concrete upright of which Banjo was grateful for—and he asked, "Dad, what's me mam goin' to say? I mean you told her it was only going to be a pound. Five-fifty! Phew!"

Denis smiled at his son's concern. "Do what Banjo does, grin and say nowt."

"But what if she asks?"

"She might not."

"But what if she does?"

Denis had a problem. It was hardly the thing for a parent to encourage his son in the telling of untruths and he said after some thought, "Well, it's a matter of degree what you mean when you say 'about a pound'. Someone who's right poor might think a pound an' tenpence was too much, but someone very rich wouldn't quibble at fifty quid. We're neither poor nor rich so I think we can call five-fifty about a pound, eh?"

For Banjo, Paul would have been willing to call a thousand about a pound, and he digested this little bit of mild jiggery-pokery for further use with variations on a theme.

The vet had told them to be careful who they let Banjo mix with until he had had the second part of the preventative injection in two weeks, and for fourteen days he chafed at the end of his lead and was forbidden to make any new dog acquaintances by his master who drove away any likely carriers of distemper with blood-curdling shouts.

Banjo did not like being under arrest, even if it was protective custody, but his wiles were not sufficiently developed to outwit his family who made sure the door was never left open nor the knot improperly secured when he was out on the rope.

But his confinement ended with another objectionable needle pushed into his hide and he regained his periods of freedom to run in the parks. The second visit to the vet's provided no embarrassing adventures involving the invasion of women's skirts but there was a short-lived pandemonioum when Banjo and the other two dogs present scented the white mouse a small boy was carrying in a wooden box. The only effect the clamouring of the would-be assassins had was to keep them sitting in the waiting room a while longer as the nurse decreed that the cause of the excitement ought to be removed and the little boy was sent into the surgery three places before his turn.

"Now look what you've done," Paul said sternly, but Banjo just grinned—and said nowt.

The first time he was allowed to run freely he acted, as Paul said later, like summat let loose. Which was what he was. Nothing irks a dog more than confinement and Banjo exhibited his joy by tearing about the park and disappearing into the distance. All Paul's threats and entreaties had no effect in making Banjo return to the captivity of the lead so Paul set off after him at a trot.

He ran through the copse into which Banjo had vanished, out the other side, but there was no sign of the escapee. There was an area of grass with a children's playground in the centre, trees on the other side and beyond the trees the railway line. The railway lines. Paul started to run again. He dodged around the swings and the see-saw and almost collapsed into the barred wooden fence dividing the property of British Rail from that of the Corporation. He could see clearly along both directions of the line and to the embankment on the other side. No Banjo. A railway worker was coming towards him, slowly as though inspecting the track. Paul ran along his side of the fence until he was within shouting distance.

(60)

"Hey!"

The man looked up and put a cupped hand to his ear. "Yer, wot?"

"Have you seen a dog?"

"Ah've seen thousands."

"I mean just now."

"What sort is it?"

"It's got a fringe."

The man guffawed. "'as it got curlers in as well?"

Paul could have fed the man, in very small pieces, to Banjo. "It's a grey dog, young with a white backside."

"'as it got a tail?"

"Yes."

The man pondered, looking back the way he had come. He scratched his chin, then his head. "Well I haven't seen it then. But I've got a left-handed pair o' braces at 'ome." Having told the joke of the year he went on his way splitting his sides.

The humour was lost on Paul. He ran back to the playground and enquired of a girl a little older than himself if she had seen a grey dog with a fringe. The girl was working a swing up to maximum speed and shouted as she kept flying by him, "Don't talk daft, dogs don't have fringes."

"This one has."

"Well it must be daft like you, then. Our dog hasn't got one."

The unhelpful people he was meeting made Paul uncharacteristically irritable. "You don't have to have a fringe to be daft," he said crossly and set off back the way he had come in the hope that Banjo was there looking for him. Banjo was not and Paul began to despair. His dog had gone out of sight before but never for very long. He stayed in the park for an hour, searching, questioning, and was not too far away from tears when he admitted to himself his quest was hopeless. Banjo could be miles away by now, still chasing after whatever whim had sent him haring off like a greyhound out of the trap. The only hope now was that whoever found him would either look at his name and address on the disc attached to his collar or hand

(61)

him in at the R.S.P.C.A. The R.S.P.C.A.! That was it, his next job, telephone the R.S.P.C.A., and there was a kiosk on his way home.

The woman who answered him took his name and address, a description of the dog, then asked how long it had been missing.

"Over an hour, now," Paul informed her anxiously.

There was a short heavy silence. "Don't you think you ought to have waited a bit longer to see if he turns up? He can hardly be classed as missing after an hour, can he?"

No one could see the gravity of the situation and Paul's voice raced with desperation, "But he's run away from me in the park an' I can't find him an' he's only young."

"All right," the woman soothed, "we've got the particulars and he'll be all right if he's brought here, but an hour's nothing to get excited about—he might even have gone home."

Paul put down the receiver with the conviction that you could not expect help from anyone in this world.

All the way home he whistled and shouted in vain and when he reached the end of his street he knew with an unshakeable certainty that he would never see Banjo's grinning face again. As he pushed open the gate, there was more than a suspicion of moisture on his lower lids and he cleared his throat harshly as he walked up the path, wondering how he would break the news to his parents without blubbering.

The reception he got when he opened the back door was not one he was expecting. Madge Holmes could be as loudly strident as any woman when the occasion demanded and her bellowing nearly blasted Paul back into the garden.

"Where've you been! An' if you're not goin' to look after that dog proper, you can take him back where you got him. You'd better not let him roam around on his own again. What if he'd got lost or run over?"

"What—"

"Never mind that! Let him out of the kennel and get that muck washed off him, God knows what he's been rolling in, dirty little midden ..."

(62)

She thundered into the living room and closed the door, probably not to have her nostrils attacked with whatever Banjo had plastered on his coat. For once Madge's shouts were ignored by Paul. Banjo was safe at home—that R.S.P.C.A. woman must know a thing or two about dogs—and that was all that mattered. Paul flung open the kennel door and Banjo shot out at him like a released, affectionate spring. Paul reared back from the welcome. Banjo stank atrociously, the odour being caused by his right side which was caked in something unspeakable.

"Get down!" Paul yelled, "Come on, in the yard while I get a bucket of water. You stink like the sewage works."

But Banjo just grinned and wagged his tail harder as he was tied to the rope to await being deluged with a succession of buckets of water and scrubbed, from a distance, with a sweeping brush.

Chapter 4

(4)

The old song, *One Man And His Dog*, might have been parodied to suit Paul and Banjo. One Boy and His Dog, and Madge's earlier description of Banjo and her son was apt, Me An' My Shadow. They were together constantly.

Paul had no training as a dog handler and didn't even know that clubs and schools devoted to the teaching of handlers existed, but he fumbled along in roughly the right direction. Because he was more his father's than his mother's son, he never hit Banjo and Banjo never developed any kind of fear of him, not the slightest timidity, knowing that if he was given anything it would be a pat, a stroke or better still a titbit. Therefore, whenever Paul called him, Banjo couldn't help responding. It didn't happen all at once, overnight, but by the time Banjo was fully grown it was a fact of life that when Paul shouted, Banjo returned. By the accident of Paul's kindly nature, they had mastered one of the most important commands, the recall.

Banjo also learned to sit at the order. The recall and the sit were the sum total of his knowledge, but the two orders were always sufficient for their needs; the boy and the dog understood the relationship of master and the mastered, the feeder and the fed, the captain and the crew.

When Banjo was two years old he was a fine healthy animal. Ungainly he may have looked with his long, stalky legs, his short, thick barrel of a body with the Banjo trademark now more clearly than ever defined, but the eyes peering through the long fringe were always sparkling bright with energy and fun. What pleased Paul most of all was the deceptiveness of his clumsy appearance and the way his comic expression could change to ugly menace in the face of a threat.

On the occasions when several owners took their dogs to exercise in the park at the same time, and the dogs for a brief time reverted to the customs of their ancestors and ran in a pack, it was always Banjo who took the lead position and therefore directed the course of the chase. The fond owners of the Labradors, Collies and Dachshunds would congregate to chat and boast of pedigrees and what they had spent in vets' fees and Paul would stay aloof, knowing nothing of dogs except what he had found out by making mistakes in the rearing of Banjo.

But for Paul the true test came when it was time to go home. He would shout just once, "*BANJO!*"

Whatever was going on, Banjo would turn in the middle of it and lollop back to his master whilst the owners of the pedigree dogs would follow their reluctant pets shouting threats or entreaties according to their natures. Paul would clip on the lead and proudly march Banjo out of the park.

For the pet of a working class family, Banjo could have asked for no happier life. He had flourished on his diet of whatever the family were eating and although his coat was of the rougher, shaggier type it shone brightly. After his booster inoculation, he had never had cause to be taken to the vet again and the few mild stomach upsets he suffered were cured by whatever remedy the local pet shop advised. Madge and Denis were both pleased that their son could derive so much lasting pleasure for such a small cost. Banjo had grown on them too. He would obey either of them as readily as Paul and where, at first, Madge had referred to him as 'our Paul's dog', Banjo became simply 'our dog'.

One October evening when Denis came home from work, his smile and 'hello' to his wife were not quite so spontaneous as usual. Paul did not notice but Madge did. She said nothing until Paul was in bed, Banjo was lying on the hearth rug with his chin on his paws and she was pouring the final cup of tea.

"Denis," she said in the voice she reserved for when either of her men were ill or in need of sympathy, "what's up, love?"

Denis looked up surprised from the evening paper. "Nowt, why?"

Madge gave him his tea and took her place by the fire. She kept her eyes on him the whole time and when he shifted his eyes to fold up the paper, she knew she was right. After fifteen years of close scrutiny, he had no more chance of keeping anything from her than the cow had of clearing the moon.

She said in a voice so gentle it would have flabbergasted her bingo pals, "Come on, love, you might as well tell me now as later an' have me worrying."

Denis carefully finished folding the paper, placed it in the magazine stand and sighed. "I've been offered another job."

"Another job?"

Denis was a highly-skilled instrument maker and it was assumed he would remain with the only firm for which he had ever worked until he retired. The promotion to manager had been promised him when the present man in charge took his retirement pension in about fifteen years' time.

Denis sighed again. "Aye, but it means movin' away from here."

Madge sat up, interested. "Where to?"

She had visions of London or Kent or Devon or somewhere equally romantic.

"Australia."

"*Australia?*"

Denis nodded and Madge sat in impatient expectancy. "Come on, then, tell me about it."

Denis's firm had been taken over by a larger company, an international concern, and applications had been invited to fill the position of factory manager at a new works near Brisbane. Two months earlier Denis had, without any real hope of success, put his name forward, but his reputation for reliability had spread wider than he knew and now he was on a short list of four from which the

(69)

new man would be chosen in the coming week.

Madge was at the same time highly elated and a little piqued. "Oh, it'd be lovely—we'd be able to see our Brenda in Sydney. You know how good she says it is out there."

Denis patiently explained that the job was not his for the asking, he would have to win it when the final selection was made, and furthermore, he was not too sure he wanted to take it. It would mean breaking Paul's education, leaving behind all their friends and family and what if they did not like Australia?

"You're too timid," said Madge firmly, "now listen to me …" When she was in that frame of mind there was no way of not listening and Denis heard all the reasons why he should grab this marvellous chance and not be an old fuddy-duddy-stick-in-the-mud.

"You do your best when they send for you. You're a good man at your job and they know it. Show 'em you've a bit o' backbone as well. Imagine me on the beach at Waikiki …"

Denis coughed. "Bondai, love, Waikiki's somewhere else."

"Well," she rhapsodised, "they're all the same out there."

Denis pushed his fingers through his hair. "I don't know," he said uncertainly. "I'll have to think about it. It's a big thing to do."

"We can do anything our Brenda and Bernard can do."

Denis wished he had not mentioned it until after the post had been filled.

At thirteen, Paul was naturally bubbling with excitement at the prospect of such an adventure. According to what he had been taught in geography lessons it was life in the sun with those wide open spaces, cattle and sheep stations and surf board riding and all the year round swimming and even ski-ing.

"It'll be great," he said to Banjo as they set off for the park, "there's millions o' rabbits for you to chase in Australia—we might even catch a baby wallaby. Better than the park."

(70)

Banjo trotted at his side, quite happy to stay where he was or go anywhere as long as Paul was with him. Paul couldn't wait to tell Puddin and the others, Puddin had said he would be going to the park to try out a model aeroplane he had built; it would be quite a change to see a gleam of envy behind those glasses instead of an 'I told you so' smirk.

The tension of excitement prevailed and dogs are quick to pick up changes in the atmosphere. Banjo did a lot more pacing about the house, as if expecting momentarily to be put on the lead and taken off to the land of his dreams.

On the morning of the interview which could change the lives of the Holmes family, Madge brushed the back of Denis's jacket, giving a torrent of advice and hints about what he should say if he was asked this or that question. Banjo was acting nervously, sitting by the door, by the window, pacing round the room for all the world as though there was something going on that he did not know about. Paul called to him to sit close and rubbed his head.

"There's nowt to worry about, they're sure to give my dad the job."

"Don't build your hopes up," Denis warned.

Madge gave his shoulder a last flick with the brush. "And don't you go into that interview with your tail between your legs. You're not *pushin'* enough, Denis Holmes, that's always been your trouble."

Denis went off to the Manchester train and his firm's head office and Paul took Banjo for his morning run on the playing fields. The turf was springier and greener, the game with the old, chewed-up rubber ball more fun, and Banjo seemed to bark more joyously; there was something tremendous to look forward to.

There would be a week's delay until the result of the interview came through, said Denis on his arrival home that evening, but the three men he had spoken to had been very informal, friendly, and they listened carefully to the way Denis thought his own little piece of the engineering industry ought to be run. He thought he was in with a chance.

(71)

They carried on, trying to be casual about it all, doing the things they always did, but under the everyday chattiness, quivered the stimulant of heady anticipation. Perhaps once in a lifetime, if it is very lucky, a working class family is offered the chance of a new life in a new country with substantial promotion and the accompanying rise in status, and the Holmeses would have been inhuman not to feel the effect. But they tried not to show it.

Madge went to her bingo three times a week. Denis had his Friday evening and Sunday lunchtime at his local, and Paul enjoyed Banjo—no more than Banjo enjoyed Paul. On the Saturday morning, they were lucky enough to see the police dog handlers working their Alsatians on the training ground they used at Temple Newsam. Paul was a little wistful that Banjo did not know how to scale a wall, do the high jump, long jump, retrieve, search, track and pull down a running criminal. But not too wistful. There was the compensation of the ready wide-mouthed 'grin' and the happy, friendly spirit twinkling out through the merry eyes behind the curtain of the fringe.

They were standing at the edge of the small wood of closely-spaced silver birch watching the police dogs go through their lessons, in line abreast at first, tracing a complicated pattern of off-the-lead heel work, then they split up to use the apparatus for jumping and scaling.

One of the handlers was a sergeant, a man very obviously experienced at the job of training dogs, whose charge looked young and not as competent as the others. The sergeant led him away across the grass to be alone where he could practise the Sendaway, the exercise which requires the dog to do the reverse of the Recall and go away from the handler in as straight a line as possible until told to drop flat. The policeman stopped fifty yards away, sat the dog at heel and gently pointed his head in the direction he wanted him to go: straight at Paul and Banjo. He stroked the dog's head, talking to him all the time, giving him confidence and then he flung up his right hand, *"Away!"*

(72)

The dog set off, running straight for ten yards before veering to the left uncertainly. Again the policeman flung up his arms. "Away! Away, Robby."

The shout was loud but jovial with no hint of remonstrance, keeping up the idea that it was all a game to be enjoyed and Robby turned his head and carried on his broken run. That was when he saw Paul and Banjo standing silently just inside the line of trees. The grey hackles lifted, the black lips worked back over the fangs and he accelerated with a sudden businesslike spurt.

Paul saw the change in the attitude of the dog, recognised the menace and whispered, "Don't move, Banjo."

It was a wasted effort. Banjo saw a playfellow and bounded from the trees for a chasing game. The intent of the Alsatian was all too clear, so clear from its snarling mouth and stiffened hair as it sped in to attack that Paul was momentarily petrified. He had only to shout to bring Banjo back but his brain wouldn't function and, horrified, he watched the dogs closing, one to play, one to savage. It was as well the sergeant was used to acting quickly. As soon as he saw the funny looking dog running to play with the one whose attacking tendencies—desirable as they are in a police dog—he was trying to channel into the right lines, he bawled, "*Down, Robby, down!*"

Robby dropped flat with hackles still bristling, teeth still bared and the policeman's shout shook Paul into action. "*Banjo! Banjo!*"

Banjo had only learned two orders by which he could be guided and protected but he had learned them well and he wheeled at once, running back to Paul.

"Stay, Robby," the sergeant shouted twice as he ran to his dog which was unrelentingly eager to get its teeth into Banjo's throat. He slipped the choker over Robby's head and walked him at heel to where Paul, who was all thumbs, was fumbling to fasten the spring clip of the lead to Banjo's collar. The sergeant was not over-tall for a policeman but he was very broad and stocky with a square, red face, a face with a look of amused rebuke. He stopped two yards from Paul, Robby sitting nicely and quietly at his left leg.

"Nah then, lad, you nearly lost your dog then. If this feller'd o' got hold of him ..." He shook his head, then grinned. "It's a good job you can recall him, I'll tell you."

Mentally Paul bridled a little, as he always did when people thought, just because Banjo was not a beauty queen, he was soft.

He said quietly, "Banjo can fight as well, he's not frightened," with defensive resentment.

The sergeant told Robby to stay and knelt down to have a look at Banjo, running his hand along the shaggy sides, down the spindly legs and having his cheek licked with a quick tongue.

He laughed and scruffed Banjo's ears. "I'm not runnin' him down, lad. I'd say you've got a good dog here—even if he is a bit fat. Give him a bit less grub an' he'll live longer—a dog that'd allus be on your side if you was in trouble. But," he looked directly up at Paul, "he wouldn't last a minute with that young bugger there. He's a proper sod with other dogs although he likes people. Next time you want to watch us workin', keep over near the road where we can see you. I didn't know you was here till I saw your dog come out o' the trees. Anyway, no harm done."

"How do you get a dog to do all them things yours can do?" Paul asked.

The sergeant had Robby at heel again ready to go back to work. "A lot o' time an' a lot o' patience and a bit o' knowledge. Take him to one o' the schools. They won't train your dog but they'll learn you to train him."

"I don't know where there is one. But anyway, it's too late now, we're off to Australia soon."

"Well I reckon they'll have a school or two out there as well. It's worth it."

"Who would have thought," Paul said to Banjo as they went to the bus stop, "that you could have been goin' to school all this time? *You* might have been able to do all them things by now. Anyway, we'll find out about it as soon as we get off the ship at Brisbane."

(74)

Banjo barked at a tattered, lethargic crow and grinned when the crow flapped into the air with a truculent caw.

It was Saturday, fish and chip day, titbit day at the fish shop, whelks-at-the-shellfish-stall day and scrag-end day at the butcher's and Banjo's eyes had the Saturday brightness, twinkling, impossibly, even more than on any other day. Being the pet of a regular customer at food shops which valued regular customers paid off handsomely and made Saturday one long lip-smacking day of heavenly pleasure.

There was also the petting from acquaintances that had grown steadily on the trips to the market and Saturday was pampering and pandering day, too. He was stroked and given sweets and spoken to and even kissed by the old lady who had lost her terrier when Banjo was young, a Mrs. Mountain, who always told him what a lovely boy he was and how much she would like to have him sleeping at the bottom of her bed in case of burglars.

Paul would look down at him and say, "They might think you look funny at first, but you allus grow on 'em in the end."

That weekend dragged for Paul. It dragged for his parents equally as they waited for Monday to hear the decision but, being adults, they were able to look calm and nonchalant even though they were as excited as Paul. Whenever Paul started to look at the map of Australia in the encyclopaedia, to compare distances and climates, he was told to take it easy and not build-up his hopes. Denis had not got the job yet. But Paul felt sure he had and would read out that Brisbane was in Queensland, about five hundred miles from Sydney.

Monday's before-tea walk was a hurried affair, a quick trip to the neighbouring streets so Banjo could choose a lamp standard and back home at the double to be there when Denis got in from work.

"He's late, mam," Paul complained.

"Only five minutes. You could be doin' your homework or something. Give up natterin', he'll be here."

When Denis did walk in there was no need to ask if he had got the job. He tried to keep a straight face but when

(75)

Banjo reared up for a stroke and a lick he grabbed the flailing tail, pulled it gently and laughed a little self-consciously, "They said the job was mine if I wanted it, so I took it."

Paul yippeed and Madge laughed with Denis. She asked, "When do we go?"

Paul shouted, "We're off, Banjo, we're off. We might call at Cape Town an' all sorts o' places."

Banjo barked, bounced round the kitchen, shook himself and sat in the kennel doorway staring at the oven. Paul was disgusted.

"Here we are, ready to go halfway round the world an' all you want is your tea!"

Denis hung his jacket on the back of the door and started to wash his hands. "I'm a bit hungry meself—oh, and we're flyin' so you won't be seein' much of anywhere."

Madge took the casserole from the oven and filled the kitchen with scented steam. "I asked you when we go."

Denis told them about it as they ate. The new factory opened in three months' time and the bosses wanted him there a month before it did open to help with the installation of the benches and machinery. He had assured them he could settle his few affairs well inside two months and fly out whenever it suited them. They were to have a bungalow on the edge of Brisbane close to the sea and countryside and the firm would help financially with the furnishings.

"They're generous," he finished.

"If they want the best, they've got to pay," said his wife not wholly as a joke. "It's goin' to cost them a packet what with the plane fares an' the house an' furniture."

Paul wolfed his food almost as quickly as Banjo, and took down the lead from the nail behind the door.

"Come on, Banj', let's go tell Puddin."

They told Puddin who showed the awe demanded by etiquette before launching into a lecture on what to do if bitten by a snake, a platypus or a dingo. Care should be taken not to cut oneself on coral when swimming in the sea but there was no need to fear sharks as the Great Barrier Reef kept them all away from the east coast.

(76)

It was during that first week of knowing for sure they were going, when Paul's excitement was still at its highest, that he got an inkling that he was going to encounter his first real personal tragedy.

In the middle of the week, Denis had gone to the office to meet the firm's Northern Area manager to confirm he would be taking up the appointment, would not be likely to change his mind at the last minute and to finalise details for the immigration of himself and his family.

The manager was asking questions and filling in forms.

" ... and you're thirty-five, and your wife's thirty-four and your son's thirteen? Right. That's the whole of your family, Mr. Holmes?"

"Yes," said Denis, but grinning as an afterthought, "I forgot about Banjo."

"Banjo?"

"Our dog."

"Just a minute," the manager said, fingering through the papers on the desk. "I've got something somewhere about exporting dogs. It's from the Australian High Commission in London. I haven't read it properly but they're very keen on the quarantine laws."

He found half a dozen typed sheets stapled together and he leafed through them, skimming over the information, then passed it to Denis. "You'd better take it home and go through it carefully ... of course, any costs incurred in taking the dog would be your responsibility, Mr. Holmes, and from what I've seen there, it'll be quite expensive. If you're in any doubt, you'll have to get in touch with the High Commission, I know no more about it than you do. Now then, have you or any of your family ever suffered from the following diseases ..."

They had not suffered from any of the diseases he listed so the manager arranged for them to have a medical examination in the coming week and Denis left him with the feeling that they were really on their way. He pushed the folded sheets of paper to the back of his mind, he didn't like the premonition they gave him. He left them in his jacket pocket until he got home that evening, until Paul had taken Banjo for a walk.

(77)

Denis gave the fold of papers to Madge. "You'd better read that, love."

She looked at him as she opened them out. "Not trouble, is it?"

"Read it, it might be."

She went through the pages carefully. Six were filled with the conditions and restrictions for exporting dogs and cats to Australia including a scale of quarantine charges, and there were a further two sheets of recommended shipping agents. She turned back to page five.

"Pass me that pen off the shelf." She quickly jotted down figures alongside the tabulated lists. Then she put down the pen with a frown of concern. "Do we have to pay this?"

"Aye, you can hardly expect the firm to pay for people's pets."

"Have you worked it out?"

"No."

She read out, "'Quarantine on arrival in Australia will normally be for a period of ninety days. Where animals or crates have been unloaded from the aircraft en route but where the seals remain intact the quarantine, on arrival, will be nine months. Where the seal has been broken the animal will be refused entry into Australia and must be returned to the country of origin, or elsewhere out of Australia.' And it says here we might have to wait months to get him into quarantine. And then it'll cost one seventy-two a day while he's in quarantine—that'll be Australian dollars, I suppose, and that makes it a hundred and fifty-four dollars at the least. How much is a dollar?"

"There's about two to a pound, I think."

"That's *over seventy-five pounds*, then, and three times that much if they unload him anywhere on the way. Over two hundred."

Denis said so quietly it was almost a sigh, "And that doesn't include his fare."

Madge looked up sharply from going over the figures again. "And how much is *that*?"

Denis did not know. "We'd better write to one of them

(78)

shippers an' find out quick ... what are we goin' to do if we can't afford it?"

Madge, as ever, was level-headed and practical. "I think I love Banjo as much as you and Paul do but we've got to keep it in proportion. He *is* only a dog and we're talkin' about our future—and Paul's more than ours."

Denis sat for quite a while staring at the television screen, and he sighed again, a sigh of feeling for his son more than himself. "Well, let's write to the shippers to find out an' we won't say owt to Paul until we know for sure. One way or the other."

Madge Holmes nodded. "Pass me the writin' pad an' I'll do it now."

Although the Post Office had made the last collection of the day, Denis went out to drop the letter in the box as soon as Madge had sealed the envelope. He heard it hit the bottom with a faint but cheerless smack and he could not shake off the feeling or foreboding at what news the answer would bring and a sense of guilt at the way Paul might be hurt. But, as Madge had said, Banjo was only a dog and their future was at stake. This was one of the few occasions in the life of Denis Holmes when he wished passionately that he was a wealthy man.

As that week passed and brought the day of leaving closer, Paul's excitement grew. He laughed quickly at nothing and was more ready than ever to do a small chore or go on an errand. He talked a lot to Banjo as if the dog were human and Banjo would grin back as though he understood every word and was sharing Paul's happiness. He and his parents had passed the medical examinations without any problems, the seats were booked for them and his father had arranged with his brother to sell off the furniture as soon as they had gone and send the money to Brisbane. The money would be important for furnishing the new home.

Paul knew this, and decided to help by saving every penny of his pocket money to pay for Banjo's food for the first few weeks. His mother would not want to take the money but he would make her, arguing that Banjo was his dog and he wanted to look after him. Maybe he would be able to get a part-time job after school and help out regularly until he started work. These and many other ideas went through his head, all passed on to Banjo when there was no one else about to think he was silly, and Banjo would peer through his fringe and grin.

Paul felt the change in the atmosphere a week after they had seen the doctor. Denis and Madge chatted normally as they ate the evening meal but there was something forced about them.

Paul asked, "Is there summat wrong, Dad?"

Madge answered, "We'll talk about it after tea."

"Nowt's happened to stop us goin', has it? I—"

Madge was firm, "I said after tea. Clean your plate up, and nowt's stopped us goin'."

They gave him the news as they had received it, by written word. First the letter from the animal export company in Nottingham, then the notes on Australian quarantine requirements with Madge's worked-out costs in the margin. What they were gently trying to tell him did not sink in all at once. When he looked up, his face was worried—but about the expense, not the fact that he could be going to lose Banjo.

"It's a lot o' money, Dad, but I can do without pocket money for a bit."

Denis said, "It could cost us over four hundred quid, Paul, and we can't afford it."

It began to penetrate then and they could see Paul was suffering the first flutterings of trepidation, of terrible doubt in the unbending solidity of his family. Banjo was now, to Paul, as integral a part of that family as he was himself and even with the first harsh realisation that, to his parents, Banjo was still no more than an animal to be petted, just another of a lower order, he refused to accept they they could be adamant, that they could *really* consider turning Banjo away. Forever.

Banjo was sprawled on the hearth rug, watching Paul through his thick straggle of hair as if reproachful that they were still in the house when they should have been outside in streets full of lamp posts or parks full of trees, but when Paul lightly slapped his knee Banjo jumped up to sit at his

(80)

side and rest his dark grey muzzle on Paul's thigh to have his head stroked. When the loving hand ran over his round skull Banjo sighed loudly, content.

Paul's forced grin was a ghastly stretching of the lips. At thirteen he was developing the adult habit of hiding emotions but he could no more control his voice than he could his facial expressions.

'But we can't leave him behind, can we?"

Denis cleared his throat as he fumbled for non-existent words but Madge moved quickly to sit beside her son, taking his hand and holding it with both her own.

"I wish there was another way of saying it, love. We know how much you love Banjo—we love him as well— but ... we just can't afford to take him. And another thing, it wouldn't be kind to take him."

Paul looked to where he always looked for help, to his father, his dad who could always smile slowly and sort something out. But at that moment Denis Holmes was as distressed as his son and was no more adept at putting on a face. He shook his head.

"Your mam's right, Paul. We've gone over everything two or three times and we just haven't got the money to spare. You know if we had, there's nowt I'd like more than to ..." His voice trailed off helplessly, he coughed and continued, "We'll have to start looking for another home for him—we'll find somewhere nice where he'll be happy."

Again his voice faded and Madge said quickly, over-brightly, "And you'll be able to get another dog when we get settled in."

"You said it wouldn't be kind to take him," Paul prompted, looking for any point of leverage, "how do you mean?"

"The quarantine laws," said Madge. "He'd have to go out locked up in a little crate that no one's allowed to open, he wouldn't even be able to have a walk. Then he'd be locked up in a kennel for three months at the quarantine station in Brisbane, nine months if they unload his crate anywhere on the way. He'd be pining for you all that time. It wouldn't be fair."

"I could go to see him at the weekends."

(81)

"That *wouldn't* be fair, either, love. He'd still be locked up all the time. You'll see it our way when you've had time to think about it an' when we've found somebody who'll look after him right."

Arguments and counter-arguments were crowding into Paul's mind but in the confusion he was unable to say anything at all. Without a word he went into the kitchen with Banjo expectantly at his heel, put on his coat, put on the lead and took Banjo out into the cool evening where he would be able to think. He would be able to think of something. He would *have* to think of *something*.

Chapter 5

(5)

Paul's determination to find a way of including Banjo in the journey waned as the day of departure closed on him. There was only one answer to his problem and that was money, and what chance does a thirteen-year-old boy have of raising four hundred pounds, he asked himself. But along with the dread of the parting came an inevitable resignation to fate. Yearn as he might, there was nothing within his powers that could alter the course of events; he was going to Australia and Banjo was not.

He would lie in bed in the darkness staring at the ceiling, hearing the motors of the night drivers on busy York Road with a mind that could supply no solution. He would lie staring, until the tears started and then he would sob. Tactfully his parents ignored the darkening circles beneath his eyes, nor did they try to cheer him up with a stream of forced, foolish lightheartedness. They respected his sorrow for the very real thing it was and did not resort to patronage on the usual parental grounds that he was 'only a kid'.

In the daylight hours, the sadness had to be put aside in the face of practicalities, the increasingly urgent need of finding a good home for Banjo and when they had only fourteen days left in the country of their birth, Banjo was still without a new master. There had been no interested response to the verbal advertisement spread far and wide by the Holmes family. Had he been a highly-strung prima donna of a pedigree, people might have been queueing up for him. Paul knew this, but no one wanted the odd-looking mongrel who was, Paul knew, as faithful and infinitely more loving and lovable than any canine aristocrat.

Paul saw a parallel in their cases, his and Banjo's. Because of their humble station, they were to be deprived of the one thing on earth that—according to his ancient teacher of Religious Instruction—was said to be free. The freedom to love and accept the love of another, Paul reasoned that love was *not* free. Love cost four hundred pounds and if you did not have four hundred pounds, then the world took away the love you could not pay for. This would leave a painful void that even time would never fully heal, and dumb, uncomprehending Banjo who had never harmed anything or anyone in his life would be left with a bewildered grief that he had been abandoned by his family. It had been said that dogs have short memories, that after two or three weeks with a kindly new owner, the previous well-loved master is forgotten. Paul hoped this was true but he did not really believe it. How could the patterns and routines of more than two years be erased in as many weeks?

Denis said Paul could take the last two weeks off school. There were many relatives to say goodbye to, many places to be visited for the last time, many friendly walks to be taken in the green parks and busy streets; and when there were only five days left Banjo was still without a home to go to. Two people had replied to the advertisement Denis had placed in the *Evening Post*, but only one of these had actually arrived to have a look at Banjo, and it seemed that one look was enough.

Paul wore an almost permanent frown of worry. If the terrible worst happened and not one person in all this big city would take Banjo, he would have to be handed in to the R.S.P.C.A. to see if they could place him. Admirable as that organisation is, Paul's stomach turned as he thought of Banjo fretting for him in the wire mesh kennels, a fretting that would last no more than seven days if no prospective dog owner took a fancy to him. On the seventh day, he would be led down the corridor to the room from

(86)

which the only exit for dogs was, when stiff and cold and in a sack, through the door and into the van which took them away to be incinerated. Fun loving, ever-grinning Banjo—dead.

Paul tried, successfully, to conceal his trauma from Banjo, spending every possible minute out walking or playing with the ball. In that last fortnight Paul—and his mother and father—unashamedly spoiled Banjo, giving him all the milk and food he could eat which, as with most dogs, was much more than was good for him. His short thick body got thicker with fat and his turn of foot suffered when he was running in the park with the other dogs.

On the last Saturday, Banjo's weekly day of delight, Madge gave Paul the smallest shopping list ever. They only needed food until Wednesday breakfast and at ten o' clock they would be taking off from Leeds and Bradford airport to make the connection with the flight to Australia at London. And now there were three days left for Banjo.

But Paul tried to be cheerful. They went on the bus to Temple Newsam Park an hour earlier than normal and walked all the way back to join the fish shop queue an hour late. They ate the belated lunch quickly and then walked to town with the shortened shopping list. Banjo seemed extra eager, whining his excitement as they threaded through the open-air market.

They walked slowly about the familiar alleys, colourfully lined with arrays of fruit, bolts of cloth and silk, bright plastic buckets and kitchenware. In the bustle of the afternoon shoppers, Paul kept touching Banjo's head and he sniffed, coughed and blinked many times. Less than three days. Banjo would have to go on Tuesday morning. Soon it would be less than two days, then one, and then in the aircraft, high over the city, he might be able to look down and pick out the R.S.P.C.A. building with Banjo inside it.

Banjo was tugging at the lead, stretching out his neck to sniff at the fillets of haddock, halibut steaks and herrings on the long row of stalls and as Paul watched him, so alive and inquisitive, his throat tightened unbearably and he wanted to be out of the market with all its choking nostalgia.

(87)

He said gruffly, "Come on, Banjo, let's go for the meat."

They were a few yards from the butcher's when an old, stooped figure appeared out of the queue-like throng which moved slowly up the alley. It was Mrs. Mountain and Paul took her arm to help her up the single step into the shop.

"Hello, love," she panted, "ta. An' how's my lad?"

Banjo knew that Mrs. Mountain's shopping bag always contained some delicacy regarded highly by dogs and was allowed to put his nose inside the open zip fastener, a little accomplishment for which he always received an unconvincing scolding and was made to sit to attention and wait for the titbit. This small ritual always took place whenever they happened to meet Mrs. Mountain and seeing it for the last time brought the lump back to Paul's throat. The old lady took a chocolate biscuit from the bag and as Banjo disposed of it, she smiled at Paul. She was old and unsteady, watery of eye but with the shrewdness of many years of living.

"Summat wrong, lad?" she asked.

Paul swallowed and nodded. As the queue moved around the shop, he told her and her face softened with sad sympathy.

"Oh hell. What'll you do, then?"

Paul didn't know what he would do other than take Banjo to the animal shelter if no new home was forthcoming before Tuesday.

"Oh, hell," she repeated. "We can't let that happen, not to Banjo—can we, lad?" she added and bent to pat his head.

Banjo grinned and eased his head in the direction of the shopping bag, hoping the stroking was a prelude to another biscuit.

"Next," said the butcher pointedly and it was Mrs. Mountain's turn to be served.

She said to Paul, "I'll see you outside, we'll have to think o' summat."

Paul almost smiled for the first time that day. Maybe Mrs. Mountain knew someone who was looking for a dog. As he was being served, he watched her through the window, afraid he would lose sight of her in the crowd but

(88)

she stayed close to the glass and when he and Banjo joined her she said, "Let's have a cup o' tea."

There was a stall where tea was served in paper cups to be drunk in any odd corner the drinker could find in the crowded alleyway and Mrs. Mountain put down her bag, leaning against the wall with a sigh.

"I feel as though I'm gettin' a year older every day." She sipped the steaming tea and closed her eyes for a moment. "Now then," she said, "what are we goin' to do about this here dog?"

Paul liked the 'we' she used. It was good to have an ally. "I don't know. We've asked everybody we know but no one wants him. D'you know of *anyone*?"

She held her white, boney hands round the warmth of the cup, sipping more tea. "I'm *sure* I know of someone. *Me*. I'd love to have him. Thing is, I don't know if I can afford him."

Paul's heart leapt as he said quickly, "I'm not *sellin'* him. I—"

Mrs. Mountain laughed at the misunderstanding. "I know you're not *sellin'* him. I mean he's not a little dog and I'm on the pension, I might not be able to feed him proper."

Paul said quickly, "He doesn't eat much—well, I mean he just has a bit of what we have, nowt special. He likes taties or fish an' bread an' soup. Owt that's left over."

Mrs. Mountain bent with difficulty to run her hands along Banjo's sides and straightened up again with a hand pressed to her back, "He seems to be doin' all right on it. Y'know, years ago, afore all these tinned dog foods, that's all any dog ever got was left overs an' if there wasn't any left overs, they got nowt. They seemed to manage all right on what they could scrounge." She stopped suddenly and then said, "I'll have him!"

She said it loudly, triumphantly, as if rejoicing that her need for companionship had overcome the necessity of watching her purse and eking out the pension, of never-ending thrift at the cost of a little happiness.

Now Banjo's chance was here, the threat of his imprisonment removed, Paul found it hard to believe. In the past

(89)

weeks he had, subconsciously, accepted as an inevitable fact that he would have to make the heartbreaking journey back from the R.S.P.C.A., to leave Banjo there with little hope of any future while he flew off to a marvellous new life in the sun. The proverbial load was lifted from his shoulders and all the joy of impossible relief was in his grin.

"D'you really mean it?"

He was not questioning the honesty of her offer, it was merely a reflexive statement thrown out by his tumbling mind. Mrs. Mountain groaningly bent again to cup Banjo's face, push the fringe aside with her thumbs and look into his eyes.

"Course I mean it. We'll be all right. I'll cadge all the neighbours' odds an' ends for him. He won't starve. Just look at them eyes! Who could see *him* locked up?"

The unhappiness of the final parting would return but at that moment it was relegated to near oblivion by this last-minute lucky escape and Paul scribbled the old lady's address with a small piece of pencil on the corner of a discarded cigarette packet.

"I'll bring him on Tuesday afternoon, then?"

An equally delighted and adventurous-feeling Mrs. Mountain nodded vigorously. "Aye, an' bring owt that belongs to him, toys an' his feedin' bowl an' his rug if he's got one. He'll feel more at home then till he gets used to me an' my funny old ways."

Paul restrained himself from hugging and kissing the old lady when they parted, he to hurry home with the news and she to go and make a place for Banjo.

Banjo woke with the dawn as he always did. He stretched his right hind leg, his left hind leg as he yawned widely, he shook himself vigorously, lapped refreshing water from the bowl and did his tour of the ground floor.

The familiar shapes of the furniture were altered by two piles of packed boxes and cases. The shelves and walls had been stripped of ornaments and pictures, the kitchen cupboards emptied, the pots and pans all carefully wrapped and placed in the boxes, changes which made Banjo uneasy. Banjo liked the sameness of habit. He liked things to be where they always were, he liked to be taken for his walks at the right times. The beloved routines had been changed lately, Paul putting on the lead and taking him out at all kinds of odd times. Not that he objected to that, but one of the greatest joys was greeting Paul when he came home from school, and as Paul did not go to school he could not be greeted on his return. These changes did not worry Banjo much but he was not quite as settled and secure as he used to be. Sometimes he woke in the night and did an extra round of the living room and kitchen, just for something to do, prodded by instinct to see that all was well.

There had also been a lot of visitors to the house, people Banjo had seen before on odd occasions, and there had been some weeping amongst the females—Madge had done a lot of weeping in the last few days. Banjo didn't know what the sobbing sounds actually meant but he could sense when his family was distressed, and when the men talked with loud heartiness as the women wept he would go quietly to sit at Paul's leg, look out through the fringe in cocked-headed puzzlement. He had liked it better before the rooms had been changed.

He went into the kitchen to poke his head into the empty cupboards which still held the faint smell of food although Madge had washed them all thoroughly. She was always washing or polishing something lately, squirting the furniture with the nasty smelling sprays and rubbing and rubbing. There were many much more interesting things to do than foul the air with unattractive smells and spend hours looking through piles of old papers, impatiently sending Banjo away if he put his questing nose in too far.

When he heard the alarm clock overhead, he spun and ran to the staircase door to meet Denis who was always first down. But there again, even that changed. This morning it was Paul.

"Come on, Banjo," said Paul, "Let's have a quick walk before they come down."

They had a quick walk to which Banjo did not object but that was yet another change in the orderly life, another precedent set.

Breakfast that morning was an exceptional feast with cornflakes and milk, crisp rashers of bacon, an egg firmly fried, all cut into convenient mouthful size and all covered with fried tomatoes and topped with a very crisp slice of fried bread. Banjo breakfasted as though he had been starved for a week, crunching the bacon rind and fried bread, gulping the egg and lapping up the tomatoes. This was another change in the morning ritual that did not displease him at all. He finished eating first, as always, and went as always to sit in his doorway to watch the food being lifted from plate to mouth, to ogle the jaws working on the food, to envy the bobble of Paul's adam's apple as he swallowed the food. He was ready for Madge to say: "You've had yours, greedy guts, go lay down!" but instead she said: "I've had enough, come on, Banjo!"

Banjo hesitated. He had half-turned at her first word. He stood on in the doorway, unsure, and Madge laughed as she put her plate on the floor.

"Come on then, dozy, don't you want it?"

Banjo wanted it, he might not have been fed at all the way he licked her plate clean and that was not the end. Denis put down his plate—with not too much left on it—and Paul broke up a slice of bread and butter to go with it. Having cleared off all the remains, Banjo went to sit at Paul's leg, nose stretched up to the table edge as he sniffed in the last of the fried bacon scent. Denis shook his head.

"There's no fillin' that dog. Good job we've got some stuff to help this Mrs. Mountain out for a bit."

When Madge started to clear the table, Paul took Banjo out. They walked quickly to the bus stop and the bus took them to Temple Newsam but they did not stay long. One quick run amongst the trees and they were on the bus again, passing their home stop, into town, around the market, through Woolworth's and Marks and Spencers, up Briggate and down Eastgate, through the big flats on the route they took home on Saturdays. Paul was talking all the time, Banjo had never known him so garrulous but he didn't use any of the words Banjo recognised. Banjo trotted happily at his side, glad to be out and doing things instead

(92)

of having to listen to the sound of the hated vacuum cleaner and Madge telling him to get out of the way.

When they got home, Banjo started to drink the water in his bowl but Madge took it from him, putting it down again filled with milk and squatting close to him as he drank. Denis had on his coat and there were two suitcases standing by the door.

He said to Paul, "Come on, son, we might as well get it over with. Get his stuff ready."

Paul silently rolled up Banjo's rug, put it in a cardboard box with his feeding dishes and the old chewed-up rubber ball; all Banjo's belongings. Banjo put his head in the box, trying to sniff out the reason for these strange actions and when he looked up Paul clipped on his lead. For a few seconds Madge hugged him before she hurried away into the living room, and then they were off again, Paul holding the lead with the cardboard box under his arm and Denis carrying the heavy cases. Paul didn't talk now, neither did Denis except to say to the man on the bus, "One and a half and a dog to Branch Road."

The bus passed through the city centre, jerking and shuddering in the slow crawl of traffic and out into the streets of houses at the other side. They left the bus at a busy junction, walking up a short hill into a street full of shops and good smells. This street, like the market and the city centre, was a street of many people, dawdling, shopping people and burdened, hurrying people. They passed several food shops but there seemed to be no time today to pause and let Banjo sniff.

They turned off the nice street into narrow streets of houses built in long rows, with no front gardens, doors opening right onto the pavement, and then they stopped at one of the doors. The doorway was a deep, brick recess with four stone steps leading up and Denis climbed the steps and knocked loudly on the door.

The old woman opened it, the old woman who met them in the market sometimes and always gave Banjo something to eat, but today she did not have a shopping bag. She wore a long old-fashioned apron with a big pocket across the front and comfortable old slippers. She opened the door wide. "Come in."

Paul and Banjo followed Denis inside and as the humans talked, Banjo made an inspection of the room. He liked visiting new places but this one was different. It was an old room impregnated with the many smells of a lot of living, smells the humans thought they had washed away but which were plain and keen to a lively dog. There were a lot of smells in the rug spread out in front of the open fire. It was not a wool rug like the one Banjo lay on at home, it was made of many pieces of cloth in many colours and it was wonderfully dusty and interesting, a rug full of character as far as a dog was concerned. There was a mouth-watering smell coming from an iron cupboard built close to the fire. It had a door of black metal with shiny bright hinges and Paul allowed Banjo to put his nose close enough to discover it was very hot. Banjo was not used to open fires. He continued his inspection of the old, highly polished furniture and the humans talked on.

Mrs. Mountain was saying, not without embarrassment: "You shouldn't have done."

Denis was unpacking the cases, stacking packets of biscuits, corned beef, tins of food, soup, beans in piles on the table. "You're welcome, Mrs. Mountain, they'll be a help an' we wouldn't be takin' it with us anyway. Not to Australia."

"Well, it's right nice of you, an' it will come in handy."

"And here's a new disc to go on Banjo's collar."

The room was not big and Banjo finished his tour with a look under the old stone sink in the corner by the window. He turned to Paul to let him know everything worth seeing had been seen and he was ready to go whenever Paul was. Paul knelt down, putting his arms around Banjo's neck, squeezing tight. Banjo didn't like this and he struggled to get free, so Paul released him, stood up, passed the end of the lead to the old woman and almost ran from the room slamming the door closed. Denis had also gone. Banjo yelped and leapt at the door. He didn't want to be left behind. So hard did he leap that the end of the lead was snatched from the old woman's hand but she didn't try to retrieve it. She stood, an ancient, bent figure, watching

Banjo whining at the door with an infinity of sad understanding in her watery eyes.

Banjo whined, he yelped and barked, crouched to try to see under the door but the gap was too small although he could plainly smell where Paul and Denis had passed over the threshold. He barked again, twice, loudly, running his nose up the edge of the door to the handle where he picked up Paul's scent again. He stayed at the door a long time, barking for Paul to come back for him and when Paul didn't come, he lay down with his muzzle on his paws, nose close up to the crack at the bottom of the door so he would catch the first scent of Paul returning.

The winter night was coming down and Paul hadn't come back. The old lady drew the curtains, put on the electric light and still Banjo lay at the foot of the door, waiting, waiting.

There was one sound guaranteed, in normal times, to bring Banjo running, the sound of milk being poured into his bowl. Milk and water have a different pouring sound and Banjo's bowl transmitted the sound in a way no other vessel did. The old woman poured some milk and Banjo heard but he was neither thirsty nor hungry.

Mrs. Mountain said coaxingly, "Come on, Banjo love, come an' have some milk."

Banjo wanted Paul. He turned to look at her but stayed where he was at the door, wanting to be there with a welcome when Paul came back for him.

There was a very old television set in the corner by the fire—everything in that house was incredibly old—one of the few luxuries the old woman could afford but that evening it didn't occupy her mind very much. She sat at an angle so she could see Banjo easily as he stuck to his vigil at the door.

She often talked to him in a quiet soothing voice. "You belong to me now, Banjo, an' I'll look after you—an' you'll look after me when you've lived here a bit. We'll be good pals, me an' you, a funny lookin' dog an' a funny lookin' old woman. I've told the missus next door and that one across the street to throw nowt out, they've to keep all the left overs for you now. We'll be all right!"

The only word he knew was his own name, looking up each time she used it, then turning his nose back into the slight draught coming under the door, the draught that would carry warning of Paul's coming so he would be ready to pounce on him as he came in the door.

At eight o'clock when Banjo had been at the door for four hours, he changed his position. He sat up and whined. It was not the same tone of whine he had been using all evening, a plaintive one of longing, the equivalent of a human wail; this was a whine of urgent need. He looked from the door to Mrs. Mountain and back to the door. He whined again. He barked once, whined again and Mrs. Mountain smiled.

"All right, I know what you want. But you've to be a good boy, no runnin' away!"

She bent to put on her shoes and as she fastened them Banjo left his post, running round the table to stand head down watching her.

She said, pretending to be severe, "Take your time, you can wait another minute. I don't like bein' rushed. I'm too old an' you're goin' to have to get used to me."

He trotted to the door and back three times before she had her coat on. With her wrist through the loop of the lead and Banjo poised, ready to be off, she said, "No pullin' now! I don't want to finish up flat on me back."

When the door started to open, he tried to dart off through the widening gap but she was ready for him, slamming the door and hauling back on the lead.

"I've warned you," she said.

The pressure of the collar on his throat made him cough and when he had finished coughing she started to open the door again, holding tightly to the leather strap and inching the door wider. She got the door open and went down the four steps with him straining on the lead all the time. Close to the doorway was a rainwater pipe. She tied the lead round this and went back up the steps to lock the door. Banjo made use of the pipe, and then they were off on their first walk. They went down the street to where the shops, locked up and dark now, still emanated the good smells.

Mrs. Mountain scolded him a little, "You're goin' to

(96)

have to slow down to my speed, lad, I'm not a youngster. Steady!"

She took him across the road, up and down the streets of houses to get him used to his new territory, talking, talking, sometimes comforting, sometimes scolding him for pulling; but now he had been able to relieve himself, Banjo was looking for Paul.

His searching nostrils tried to pick up Paul's scent on the air and on the ground but Paul had not been this way recently. If he had, his unforgettable scent would be there to be found. They went back home, Mrs. Mountain taking no chances and tying him to the rainwater pipe again until she unlocked and opened the door.

Banjo stayed by the door, sitting, lying, restless for Paul to come for him and take him home, occasionally whining in his unhappiness. Mrs. Mountain watched him more than she watched her old television set with its dim picture, feeling for him as dog lovers do when an animal is fretting, knowing the only cure for Banjo, as for humans when faced with a personal loss, is time. Less time for a dog than a human, for dogs have shorter memories and are, in a way, more practical, living for the minute. Soon, in a day or two, he would settle down to be her dog, with Paul a fast fading memory as his interest was taken with the new surroundings, walks that were strange to him, the new canine friends he would make. But until he attached himself to her, as he surely would, she would have to take great care. Ten days was her firm opinion, ten days and Banjo would own her as surely as she owned him. She smiled, secure in her certain knowledge of dogs. Ten days it had taken Bambi the terrier to become her dog after the death of his original owner and ten days it would take any dog.

Banjo liked Mrs. Mountain, called Emily by her neighbours, because she had the same inherent kindness as Paul. On his third day with her he took to watching the door from a lying position on the old clip rug at her feet while she watched the television. That was in the evenings when the longing for Paul was strongest, when the brown eyes under the fringe were full of hurt pleading. The daytimes were not so bad.

He missed his free running in the parks, often forgetting he was on the lead and starting to bound off after the other chasing dogs, but Mrs. Mountain would hold on tightly and tell him, "Soon, Banjo, soon. You'll be runnin' about again in a bit."

His unused energy increased inside him like a time fuse and consequently he put on fat as his body built up reserves of food.

His new routine consisted of a ten-minute walk before breakfast, later on a prowl around the house as Mrs. Mountain cleaned and dusted, a walk to the shops before lunch, a quiet hour after lunch when Mrs. Mountain dozed, a walk in the nearby park followed by another of Mrs. Mountain's dozes, and the long evening after tea. They went out once after tea in the late evening just for a few minutes, and when they came back she carefully locked and bolted the door for the night.

One change Banjo did like was that he was allowed upstairs to the only bedroom. Not only allowed but led to where his own rug was placed close to the foot of the bed. Mrs. Mountain wanted the security of his presence in a world full of burglars and muggers, and although the yearning for Paul was still strong in him, Banjo liked to be close to her. She was not Paul but she was *someone* and Banjo was as gregarious as any of his kind.

In those first three days Emily Mountain often used the two words of command learnt by Banjo until he reacted to them as quickly as if Paul had given them. When she said 'sit' he sat, and when she said 'Banjo' loudly, he would come to her and was always rewarded with a piece of biscuit for 'being a good boy'.

"You're learnin' quicker than Bambi did," she said with great satisfaction both at Banjo's apparent acceptance of his new life and the confirmation of her knowledge of dogs. Dogs were uncomplicated, simple, easy to manipulate if you showed them they were loved.

Indeed, in the close confines of the small house where everything was permeated with Mrs. Mountain's scent and everything was so different from his own house, it was impossible for Banjo not to have his mistress in the forefront of his mind. She it was who fed him, watered him, stroked him, took him for walks and, most important, loved him. Not that Banjo understood love as an emotion but any dog will feel some affinity to whoever is constantly feeding him pieces of biscuit and chocolate, and will eventually attach himself to them.

Mistakenly Emily Mountain credited Banjo with the capacity of deep understanding and probing intelligence possessed by no animal other than the human species. On the fourth day she really believed he would, by this time, have reasoned that Paul had gone for good and that his permanent home was here in the district of Armly. Because of her enormous belief in the workings of animal minds, she started to make mistakes and she made the first one on that fourth day. She took Banjo shopping in the market.

They got off the bus at a stop Banjo was not used to, but he had known where he was, near the place of plates of whelks and tossed pieces of meat, before the bus pulled up. It was the proper day, too, Saturday, exactly one week since his last visit to town with Paul, so Paul would be there at the shellfish stall or the butcher's or wandering up and down the alleys.

Mrs. Mountain saw the change in him, the quickening eagerness as they threaded through the streets to the top entrance of the huge covered bazaar and she read it wrongly. She took the brightening of eyes, the nervous spring of his step as pure joy for being back in a place he knew. In his nervousness he had to relieve himself twice on the way to the market, once against a wall and once against the wheel of a parked bicycle—to Mrs. Mountain's mortification—and she quickly pulled him away before the owner of the bicycle emerged from the shop.

"You haven't to do that in town," she hissed at him as she hurried into the anonymity of the grinning window shoppers.

A fat man considerately held open the swing doors of the market for them and Banjo was enveloped in that glorious mixture of smells and the shouts of the salesmen. His nose was bombarded with the smell of fish, fowl, game, meat, fruit, cloth, spices, herbs, soap and the blended scent of hundreds of people. Hundreds there might be to mask Paul's individual scent, all mixed up with the aromas of the merchandise, but Paul would be here and Banjo would find him.

He lifted his head to sniff with quick short inhalations and Emily said, "You *do* like it here, don't you, Banjo?"

Banjo never stopped searching as his supposedly short memory conjured up pictures of happy times, countless Saturdays with Paul and he did not despair—not until they had been to his friend the butcher, the last call, and were on their way out into the street again. Then he felt the first panic and started to pull on the lead.

Mrs. Mountain tightened her hold and said as she would to a discontented child, "Now that'll do. We can't stop here all day. We'll go to the park later on."

As they passed the glass doors of Woolworth's he tried to see if Paul was in there but there were too many people going in or coming out. They only stopped at one other shop, an interesting one with heaps of pies and cooked meats, but the people behind the counter didn't know Banjo and threw him nothing to eat. Then they were waiting for the bus, on the bus going home to the old house that was not home yet to Banjo, but he sat quietly looking through the window with eyes from which some of the brightness had gone again. It was taking a long time to find Paul.

That evening, Emily Mountain could see Banjo was much more settled. He did not prowl so much and spent more time lying at her feet, sometimes putting his nose into the clip rug and sniffing and she thought, "It's not going to take even ten days with this one." Her smugness in her knowledge of dogs led her into the second mistake.

When they went to the park next day, Sunday, it was much quieter than usual, most of the owners making the dogs wait for a run while they enjoyed a long lie in. There was no pack of pals running about on the grass. Banjo was pulling at the lead, trying to get under a low bush to see what there was to see and Mrs. Mountain thought it was safe enough now. He knew where he lived and who he belonged to.

"Banjo!" she said firmly.

Obediently he left the intriguing bush and stood at her side. She looked into his eyes, "You will be a good lad if I let you have a run while it's quiet, won't you? You won't start fightin' if any other dogs come? No, course you won't. All right then, but not for long, just a few minutes this first time."

She unclipped the lead, giving him a little push, "Go on then, have a play about."

Free to move as he wished for the first time in five days, Banjo exploded into a cavorting, twisting run that took him a hundred yards away from Mrs. Mountain almost before she could open her mouth.

She shouted "Banjo, Banjo, come here!"

Banjo raced and turned, turned again, charged and sprinted, barked, nearly crashed into a tree trunk and took not the slightest notice. She shouted again and again repeatedly but he was blind and deaf to everything but his freedom to run.

For ten minutes he flew about on the grass at top speed and then the old woman's frantic shouts penetrated. He stopped to look at her across a distance of a hundred and fifty yards. When he stopped, she started towards him.

"Come here, Banjo!"

But Banjo was free, really free to go and find Paul and he would find him in one of the places they always went. He turned his rump on Mrs. Mountain and trotted away through the trees, her fading voice not registering. And she had forgotten to change the disc on his collar.

Chapter 6

(6)

The weather was good for the time of the year, bright but without the sharp nip to be expected in December, and the streets were fresh and friendly. They started, the streets, where the grass of the park ended and Banjo's claws tic-tacked smartly on the stone pavements as he trotted homeward.

He didn't know where he was, never having been on this side of the park before, but he knew which way to go and there was no faltering in his pace or changing of direction when he came to a corner or junction. He was sometimes at tangents and curves because of the geography of the streets but he always pointed his nose at the winter sun.

The steady trot put ground quickly behind him, the set of his head, the rhythmic click of his claws, the small metallic jingle of the disc on his collar and the bounce of his shaggy coat made him look like a dog who knew his way around. He stopped once to exchange barks with a fierce Alsatian penned behind the high wire gates of a factory yard and he stopped again to look down through the lattice work of the bridge at the dark, oily river but he didn't stop for long. He wanted to get home.

Some of the places he passed he remembered having seen from the bus the previous day and as he got closer to the City Square with the tall surrounding buildings, any small doubts he might have had were dispersed. Now he did know where he was. He was almost in the shopping centre, the street in front of him across the square led to the market and beyond the market was Quarry Hill and beyond that York Road and up York Road was home.

On the steps of the big round building which was the Corn Exchange sat two men. One was drinking from a bottle and the other was taking bites of something wrapped in paper. They didn't look very friendly men. The young one who was drinking from the bottle wore a long overcoat, and filthy ankles showed over the tops of his old boots; his face was pitted and dirt-stained and matted hair hung down to his collar. The old one, who was gnawing savagely into the paper wrapping, was wearing two ragged raincoats and oversized wellington boots; his face might have been pleasant but Banjo couldn't see it for hair, eyebrows and beard which merged into a tangled mask as shaggy as Banjo's coat. One pair of eyes glowered at Banjo over a bottle and a second pair over a dirty paper wrapping. Whatever Banjo may have been, he was not a defeatist; nor was he hungry but he was always ready to join anyone at the dining table. He sat on the pavement close up to the bottom step, head erect, tail thumping the flagstones, wearing his best grin. The old man chomped, the young one gurgled. They both watched Banjo warily. Banjo caught the smell of the food in the old man's mouth and shuffled forward, putting his front paws on the bottom step.

The old man said as he chewed revoltingly, "I once 'ad a dog like that."

The young one took the neck of the bottle from his mouth, belched hugely and sighed with satisfaction. "No one ever 'ad a bleeding dog like that—if it is a bleedin' dog. Looks more like a sheep or summat." He sat with the bottle resting on his knee considering Banjo, then amended, "Or one o' them llamas they 'ave in 'ong Kong or somewhere."

For a few moments they were a silent trio except for another spell of gurgling and the crackle of the newspaper wrapping. The drinker put the bottle back on his knee and belched more genteelly.

"It wants a bit o' your black puddin'."

The eater removed his mouth from the paper, chewing thoughtfully as he held the paper out to Banjo, "'ere y'are then, if yer want a bit."

His right foot was raised slightly, ready to repulse Banjo should he decide to take advantage of the offer but years of sleeping in alleys in a methylated stupor sharpen neither the wits nor reflexes. Banjo accepted the invitation with the agility which belied his clumsy appearance. Before the old man could take evasive action, Banjo had stood up and reached out in one movement, taking the paper and its contents neatly from the unready fingers. He would have eaten the food on the pavement in the presence of his benefactor but he didn't have a chance to separate the black pudding from its protection of grubby paper before the old man shouted:

"Gerroff me breakfast yer bleedin' thing!"

The words were meaningless but the tone in which they were delivered was not. The young man was hooting vulgar laughter as the old man scrambled to his feet to retrieve his breakfast but his effort was doomed. Banjo would not have taken the black pudding had it not been proffered but now it was in his possession he had no intention of making a return gesture. He snatched up the dirty, half-eaten delicacy and loped off in the direction of the market with the old man shambling after him yelling unintelligible threats.

Banjo soon left him behind, and stopped in the closed and locked market entrance to devour his snack. He liked the solidified pig's blood and he didn't leave the rubbery black skin for although it was unchewable it carried the same pleasant flavour as the pudding it had enwrapped. He gulped down the skin, licked his lips, urinated on the gates of the market, shook himself energetically and carried on his broken journey.

This was much better than being kept in Mrs. Mountain's room, comfortable as the room was, and it would be better still when he found Paul and lived again the life he loved. When he had skirted the market, he took the route he knew so well, up through the barrack-like Quarry Hills flats and into York Road, normally a busy Clearway but now rather somnolent under the pall of Sunday morning with just the odd car droning by.

It was not far now and Banjo speeded up to a pace that

(107)

would have been a canter had he been a horse, his free swinging spindly legs carrying the compact body, with lifted head and straggling tail, with an ease that lent his peculiar form a kind of grace. Pads thudding, claws clicking, disc rattling, he swerved off the main road into the Corporation Estate and when he saw his own house he barked twice. He had come home.

The green wooden gate was standing open and Banjo charged up the asphalt path, scattering the loose granite chips as he skidded round the corner to the back door. The back door was closed. He barked and waited to be let in. The door did not open. He barked again, impatient to feel Paul's hands on him, eager to see his own kennel, to lie on the hearth rug, to be taken out, to come back, to be loved. He had no reason to believe that Paul wouldn't be here. Paul had always been here so there was no other place he could be, just as Banjo's place was in this house and always had been.

He sat outside the back door, barking periodically, scratching at the weathered paintwork. And he didn't tire. He barked and he scratched for upwards of an hour with every indication of carrying on for the rest of the day. That was until the residents of the estate took exception to having the peace of Sunday morning shattered by an unrelenting mongrel.

He stopped barking when he heard the angry voices out in the street.

"Where the bloody 'ell is it, Fred?" asked someone with headachey petulance. Fred's voice was sour with last night's considerable intake of draught Guinness.

"Back of 'olmes's ah think. Ah'm gonna kick its bleedin' 'ead in. It'll be that dog they tried to give away."

Banjo came from the back of the house to face them when he heard them coming up the path. He read correctly the purposeful, threatening stride of the leader, Fred, who wore a scowl which a stone statue could not have failed to interpret, and he went into a slight, tense crouch. He pulled back his lips and growled. Running away from the boots of an irate tramp had been the right thing to do since Banjo had won the black pudding prize

(108)

and there was nothing to fight for, but now these men were coming onto his property, his and Paul's property, and running away was out of the question. Fred came on at a slower pace, stopped when the growl turned into a fang-baring snarl and Banjo crouched lower.

The petulant one said, "Go on, Fred, give it some boot."

Fred's boots, his working footwear equipped with steel toecaps, pulled on hurriedly and unlaced gave him confidence. He drew back the right foot, bawling, "Go bark somewhere else yer mangey bastard." He swung his foot more as a threat than in a serious attempt to kick Banjo's head. But Banjo did not know that. As the foot swept higher than his head, Banjo leapt up under it, snapping at Fred's ankle. His teeth grazed the achilles tendon, clamped and locked into the trouser leg, propelling a now frightened Fred sideways into the moist soil of the garden.

Fred yelled his surprised terror as he landed in the dirt. "It's gone bleedin' barmy. Gerrit off!" Banjo held on to the trouser leg, snarling and growling through the mouthfuls of cloth, pulling back with head-shaking jerks until the cloth ripped. Fred was on his feet and down the path as Banjo pawed the cloth from his teeth.

Fred's rearguard was standing in the street watching over the prudently closed gate and Fred shouted into his face: "You're a lot o' use, pissin' off an' leavin' me to get worried." He got through the gate and slammed it shut. He was still shouting. "It's gone mad. Look at me trousers!"

The rearguard agreed. "We'd better get the police."

"*You* can get the police," said Fred, "I'm off 'ome." Fred went home, his unhelpful friend to the telephone.

Having chased away the intruders, Banjo went back to his post at the door. He barked twice quickly, tried a few more scratches at the door and lay down to wait. Sooner or later Paul would let him in and he was quite comfortable lying there in the sunshine. He even dozed off.

It was the scrape of the gate latch that woke him. It must be Paul coming home. He got up, dashed round the corner to see another stranger coming hesitantly up the path. It was a policeman, a fresh-faced very young policeman, sent by his sergeant with a grinning assurance that anyone can handle a mad dog.

"Now then," said the policeman, "you won't bite me, will you?"

He was very, very inexperienced both as an upholder of the law and as a mad-dog catcher but he had to show the group of interested spectators gathered outside the gate that the English bobby is still everyone's best friend and protector. A retrousered Fred had come along to watch and he offered some uncompromising advice.

"Give it a clout wi' yer stick, mate. Friggin' thing's cost me a pair o' strides."

One woman said, "Well, it's never bit anyone afore."

Banjo didn't like the way the policeman approached with his hands outstretched, pushing his right foot forward and drawing the left slowly over the loose asphalt.

Banjo growled low down in his throat and the policeman said over his shoulder, "It'll be better if you lot clear off, you're making it nervous."

"Nervous," muttered Fred, "I wish I 'ad a gun."

"And I," said the same woman who secretly wished Banjo had removed a substantial piece of his posterior instead of trouser leg, "say 'e's never bit anyone afore."

But no one made a move to leave the scene of the drama so the policeman got on with the job. He started to shuffle forward again and when he was two yards from Banjo he was warned with a louder growl and an initial pulling back of the lips. He took another slower step, his neck prickling warmly when Banjo started to crouch and converted the growl into a snarl. There had been nothing said at the training school in Harrogate about how far English bobbies should go in the risking of life and limb in apprehending dogs who thought they were doing their duty in guarding the property of their masters and somehow he felt he would be ragged unmercifully in the canteen if he returned with his uniform in shreds. But he swallowed his fears and smiled at Banjo.

"Come on, then," he coaxed, "I won't hurt you, will I?" But Banjo just snarled louder and crouched lower.

The policeman was also crouched, knees bent, arms

(110)

outstretched; he felt utterly ridiculous and inadequate and he didn't know what to do next. To go on was to be bitten, to give up was to project the wrong picture of constabulary to the expectant spectators. He dithered and as he dithered his salvation drove up in a small van with the words 'Police Dog Patrol' painted on the sides.

"Hey up," Fred broadcast in his thundering shout, "T' Seventh Cavalry's arrived."

The 'Seventh Cavalry' was a policeman with three stripes on his sleeve. He could see over the top of the people clustered round the gate and he grinned at the still tableau on the pathway, policeman and dog crouched facing each other. He shouldered his way through the audience.

"What yer gonna do, Reg, bite him or get him in a half nelson?"

His young colleague went pink with relief and embar- rassment as the watchers tittered at the joke and as he straightened up and relaxed so did Banjo.

The sergeant said, "Just watch an' I'll show you summat. I happen to know that dog an' it's not mad."

Nonchalantly he ambled up the path, looking anywhere but at Banjo, and as he walked he took from his pocket a bar of chocolate. He unwrapped it with a flourish, made a gesture of biting into it, chewed with relish; and Banjo was suddenly sitting, grinning, his eyes immovably fixed on the chocolate. The sergeant stopped a few feet away, snapped off and tossed a square carelessly in Banjo's direction. Banjo made a short leap, caught the chocolate, chewed it, swallowed it and returned to the sitting position.

The sergeant said, "That's a good lad. 'ave another bit."

Banjo 'fielded' and ate his other bit, sat again and the sergeant was almost on top of him. The speed with which Banjo had moved ought to have warned the sergeant that his appearance was deceptive for as he bent quickly to catch Banjo by the collar Banjo twisted away and retreated down the path.

"Oh aye," the sergeant said knowingly, "you want some more chocolate first, do you? Here y' are then." He tossed the remainder of the bar in one piece in a high curve, following it up with the intention of grabbing Banjo as he

(111)

was eating it. But through his fringe Banjo saw the move, caught the chocolate in mid-jump and ran with it to the bottom of the back garden. The sergeant stood with his fists on his hips.

"That dog's not as daft as he looks," he mused. He turned and asked of the crowd, "Can he get out through the back anywhere?"

Banjo answered the question for him by squeezing through a gap in the privet hedge and making his exit via the adjoining garden.

The sergeant took off his cap and grinned. "He's no mug, that dog, but you saw him respond to kindness," he was using the authoritative tone he used when training recruit handlers, "so if he comes round here again you've only to feed him and keep him here till you send for us or the R.S.P.C.A. And he's *not* dangerous."

"Not bleedin' much!" muttered Fred.

The primeval instinct passed down through the ages from his forebears the wolves, which can be so keen it constitutes an extra sense, had warned Banjo of the trap and he didn't want to be trapped, however well intentioned or kindly the trapper. He wanted to be free to find Paul. There were places such as the parks, the sports fields, the fish shop, the market with which Banjo connected Paul and to these places he would go and look until he achieved his aim. He paused for a few seconds to eat the chocolate and then set off for Temple Newsam Park, the place foremost in his memory. The sun was low in the late afternoon as he set off eastward, but the sky was clear and the sun a deep orange, promising another fine winter day to follow.

Not that Banjo had any interest in the weather. His heavy coat kept him warm in the daytime and at night he had his cosy kennel. He loped on following the bus route, maintaining his canter up long Halton Hill and winding Temple Newsam Road with the late golfers swinging away on the right and the deserted athletics track on the left. This was Banjo's part of the world because it was Paul's part of the world and he reached the first trees of the park with his tail erect, his head held high as he searched and sniffed.

The sun had reached the horizon when he got to the level going on the hilltop but Banjo didn't falter. He started on the circuit they mostly used, around the mansion house and along the wire perimeter fence to the ponds, and from the ponds back up through the trees.

It was fully dark when he came out of the trees onto the football pitches where he met another dog. It was a very young dog not long out of puppyhood and it was whining either with fear or misery. It was the whining which led Banjo to it and the young dog fussed around him, sniffing and licking his face as though Banjo was his long-lost brother—or more likely, mother.

There was not much of interest about the young dog; it smelled of humans and it was playful but Banjo had no time to play just then. It was dark and he had to get home to Paul and something to eat. He set off again for the glow of the city lights with the young dog trotting at his side and that was all right. Banjo didn't mind company.

All the way down the road and past the golf course the young dog made attempts to start a game going. He would bump into Banjo's shoulder and pretend to bite his neck, he would run on a few yards, turn and crouch facing Banjo in the universal opening gambit of the chasing game but Banjo ignored all his advances and ploughed steadily on. Banjo was getting hungry and the hollowness in his stomach enlarged the picture of Paul who meant food. At Halton the young dog wearied of his dour travelling companion, flopped down panting by a garden wall and watched Banjo's pace speed up on the easier going down Halton Hill. He couldn't have kept up much longer and anyway the long-legged, shaggy dog was not good company.

All the windows of the houses in Banjo's street were glowing brightly and warmly in the winter evening as the families ate or laughed or argued or televiewed and all the houses were living things because of the people inside them. All except Banjo's house. When he went through the gate which was still standing open, the age-old instinct warned him something was amiss. There were no fresh scents, on the path or around the doorways, of Paul or Denis or Madge and there were no lights in the windows to give life to the bricks and mortar.

Banjo went slowly to the back of the house, he barked just once and scratched at the door, a last sad gesture more than a serious request for he was beginning to accept the inevitable. The deadness of the house was a heavy, drear weight of gloom, more tangible to a simple mongrel dog than to the complex brain of a human which would manufacture distractions to compensate the loss. Banjo felt only the loss.

He didn't have the sophistication of thought process to help him reason that all things must end, that his time with Paul had been good and that now he must take whatever was offered to him in the way of a home and food, but he did have something else to distract him and substitute constructive effort for unhappiness; he was getting hungry and thirsty, he must find food and water.

He stood in the dark garden sadly looking at the black oblong of the back door which would not open, he whined a soft equivalent of the crying of a human and with dejection in the drooping tail and low-held head, he left his garden to look for something to eat.

The nearest place was the fish and chip shop where the man always tossed a few chips over the counter as he and Paul had queued for the order, but it was Sunday and the shop was closed, as deserted and lifeless as the house had been, it smelt of cold fat instead of crisply battered fish and steaming chips.

Images of the places he connected with food passed through his head, the next most prominent thing being the market so he set off down the yellow lighted road. He passed the pub, gay and noisy, but he had never been in there and it held no association with food or drink. He retraced that morning's journey through Quarry Hill and by the big bus station only to stop at the locked gates of the market. The smells from the fish row were strongest as they always were, but he was barred from hunting for scraps by the locked gates. Everywhere Banjo liked was inaccessible to him that night, and the one place in all that city

(114)

where he would have been welcomed—could he have found his way there—never formed itself into a picture to jog his memory. The house of old Emily Mountain.

He turned away from the market, walking slowly, aimlessly across the car park to where the lights of the bus station held out a hope of companionship.

There were plenty of people in the bus station, but they were all there for a purpose, to catch a bus, and had no time to spare for mongrel dogs so Banjo trotted the length of the colonnade, out at the other end and into Eastgate. He was getting very hungry now. All his life he had been used to eating three times a day and all he had had since the evening before was a doubtful piece of black pudding and a bar of chocolate. In the middle of the cross roads at the top of the hill he caught scent of food, the mouth-watering aroma of frying meat and onions, which he followed to the source at a dead run.

The smell was coming from a small, roofed cart with a white-coated lank-haired youth in attendance. The youth poked disconsolately at his sausages, burgers and onions with an unhygienic spoon, looking as though he wished he was elsewhere. Banjo stopped his charge, sat and grinned up at the youth. The youth glanced at him once and turned his attention back to his stirring. The smell of the hot-dogs and hamburgers, onions included, were not so irresistible that the cart was ringed by demanding customers, in fact Banjo was the only one interested at the moment in the culinary talents of the youth. Still sitting, he shuffled nearer the cart and the youth looked down again.

"Gerraway yer black-faced bastard," he said without heat. "Don't want you 'angin' around when the pictures come out, they might think I'm puttin' you in the pot next." He laughed in a high-pitched neigh at his own wit.

Banjo shuffled nearer, a ploy which, if persevered with, had often got him extra food from Madge Holmes. A blob of lighter colour in the shadow of the cart caught his eye; it was one of the bread rolls destined to enfold a sausage, dropped by accident, trodden on and kicked out of the way. Banjo preferred butter with his bread but at that moment he was one of the beggars of the world so he held it to the ground with one paw as he tore at it with his teeth.

The youth gave his delicacies another lackadaisical stir. "If you'll eat mucky bread, you *must* be 'ungry. *Our* dog wunt eat bleedin' bread, the old lady feeds him better than me."

The trodden-on roll disappeared in seconds and when the hot-dog vendor finished speaking Banjo was again sitting and wearing his best grin.

"Could y'eat another?" the youth asked and took Banjo's six-inch forward shuffle for the affirmative.

"'ere then, but don't be comin' reg'lar."

Banjo caught the roll, tearing at it as though it were prime steak and swallowing it in three voracious bites, but when he sat again, looking up through the fringe, the youth considered he had done his good deed for the day.

He jerked his thumb. "'op it, you'll get no more."

Banjo didn't know the meaning of 'hop it'. He knew the meaning of the smells coming from the cart and intended to stay in the vicinity of them. The youth ignored him.

It was not long before, as the youth predicted, people started crowding out from the nearby cinema and a little girl ran up.

"Two hot dogs and three hamburgers, please. My mummy'll be here in a minute to pay you."

"Right," carolled the youth, turning on his sales charm, "we give the onions away and they're cheap at half the price."

The little girl rewarded his effort at comedy with a giggle and with all the airs of a *cordon bleu* chef he started to make the sandwiches. He placed them in a line on a small shelf which was below the level of the cooking area of the cart. A young couple ordered hamburgers and as he went to work again the youth told his first customer:

"Go an' fetch your mother with the money or they'll be cold." She scampered away to hurry up her tardy parent and he set to work to tend the small queue.

Banjo was still watching. His insidious forward shuffles had taken him to within a foot of the cart, unnoticed by the youth who was now fully occupied, and the proximity of the food was really making the juices run. Banjo had never been so hungry, from each corner of his mouth trickled a steady flow of saliva and that hamburger on the end of the shelf was perilously close to his nose; temptingly, tauntingly close. He knew it was wrong to take food that had not been given to him but it was also wrong that he should be hungry and it was a case of which of the two wrongs was most right under the circumstances. He stood the temptation as long as he could, drinking in the flavoured air, until the demands of his basic needs ousted the command of his minimal training and he reverted to instinct. Instinct tells a dog to eat when hungry, so Banjo ate.

The shelf was so low he did not have to stretch to reach the hamburger, and the end of the roll was conveniently projecting off the end of the shelf. He had eaten the first bread rolls beside the cart because they had been legitimately acquired but perhaps there was the blood of lurchers, those princes of canine thieves, somewhere in Banjo's veins for, with the speed that had been the delight of Paul, he snatched the hamburger and was away into the cinema crowd. He heard the outrageous bawling of the youth, the laughter of those who had witnessed the robbery, and he accelerated in the direction of the market. He had to stop once to drop his prize on the ground as the meat and onions were too hot for his tongue but, at the approach of a group of noisy youths whom he saw as possible avengers, he picked it up again, bearing the heat, and disappeared amongst the cars parked on the waste ground.

Deep in the shadows of the vehicles he ate the bread first, being the coolest, then the meat, being the tastiest, and then the onions simply because they were edible and they were there. His diet at the Holmeses had fortunately made him almost omnivorous, a desirable state for a homeless, wandering dog and he would be able to eat things many dogs would not even recognise as food.

Good as the hamburger had been, Banjo's belly was far from full. The urgent need for food and water kept him effectively from thinking about Paul. But he wanted water and he knew where to find it. When he had drunk, he would look for more food. Before leaving the dark scene of his repast, he snuffled around in the dirt in case he had inadvertently dropped any crumbs. Then he gave himself a thorough shake, left the darkness of the cars, crossed the yellow lighted street and went into the shadows of the tall market building. Near the bottom gates there was a tap fixed to the wall, a tap which dripped away steadily into its grate, at just the right height for Banjo. It was a long slow job quenching a thirst at the dribbling rate and he had not really had his fill when he tired of the exercise. And he was thinking about food again.

Hunting grounds are often described as happy but Banjo's proved not to be when he returned to the hamburger stall. He went there because it was the last place he had obtained something to eat. He had forgotten the threats—remembering, as more intelligent creatures than he often do, only the good things: the bread rolls and the hamburger. Confident that the youth would again feed him, he trotted up to sit, grinning, close to the cart.

The youth was in the act of squirting tomato sauce into a hot-dog ordered by a pug-faced man who was having difficulty maintaining his balance.

"Come on, then," grumbled the customer whose aggressively out-thrust jaw did not belie his temperament. "Yer'll 'ave me missin' me bus."

That was when the youth, who was getting tired and who was not in the best of moods, saw Banjo. He turned the stream of red sauce from the hot-dog onto Banjo's face and only the protective fringe prevented Banjo from having his eyes painfully filled with the red dressing that the youth had not forgotten to dilute with vinegar, the cost of sauce being so high. The messy stream was well aimed, taking Banjo off guard and, whilst it did not temporarily blind him, the stinging vinegar had the same effect by matting his fringe into a soggy curtain. Banjo leapt back, knocking into the legs of a passer-by and earning a lightweight kick in the ribs. Unable to see, he acted on reflex and snapped at the foot that kicked him, missing the foot and hearing the youth laugh, "Go on, mate, give it some bleedin' boot. Thievin' bastard." But the

(118)

kicker had walked on and Banjo pawed at the mess on his fringe.

The waiting customer was never the nicest type of person, even when stone cold sober; after an evening of drinking several pints of strong beer he was never anything but downright nasty. He was not a lover of dogs but here was an excuse for him to demonstrate his physical superiority over the youth. The youth shouted in pain when his bicep was roughly gripped and he was forcibly turned from enjoying Banjo's predicament.

"Gerroff me—"

In the same movement the customer had taken the sauce bottle from his hand, powerfully squirting the red jet into the youth's face. The youth screamed when the sauce burned his eyes. He jerked and kicked out wildly at his tormentor who disliked being kicked at more than he disliked most things.

"Yer greasy little pratt," he snarled and smacked the blinded youth hard with the flat of his hand.

The sauce would not come off Banjo's fringe but his pawing had made a parting through which he witnessed the ending of the youth's chastisement. He saw the angry man slap the youth and then shove him forcefully against the two-wheeled hot-dog stand. It was constructed so that it had three points of contact with the ground, the wheels and a folding iron leg, all giving ample support and steadiness under normal conditions. But when the youth collided blindly and violently with the back of the cart, the cart bucked, thudded back onto the iron leg, bounced once more on the leg, shaking the holding clip loose and activating the spring which neatly drew the leg up under the body of the cart out of harm's way. The law of gravity is not only for falling apples and the cart tipped towards the floundering youth, who was engulfed in a wave of sausages, burgers, onions and the indeterminate liquid in which they were being cooked.

The store cupboard built into the body of the cart burst assunder releasing an avalanche of uncooked food. In the split second it took Banjo to credit that what he was seeing was real, two more mongrels appeared with the speed of

(119)

Jack-in-the-boxes to join the party. The youth danced about yelling his pain and the dogs darted about around his legs snatching hungrily for the food which was quickly cooling down to suit canine tastes. The youth was trying to hold his saturated trousers away from his legs as he attempted to get out of the revolting morass which his feet were pounding into pulp. Had Banjo had time, he might have rejoiced with a chorus of barks but with more food at his disposal than he had ever seen before he was busy snatching up cooked and uncooked sausages or burgers—it was all the same to him—and swallowing them with hardly a bite as he paddled about happily. With the help of the other two dogs the ruined stock was quickly disappearing.

At first the scene of the hopping youth and tomato-splashed dogs generated only laughter from the crowd which had quickly congregated but someone recognised the youth's plight as real: a fat bald-headed man with a pompous manner moved to the edge of the lake of spreading grease to wave a rolled-up newspaper at the dogs; "Go away, go on, go away."

The youth was now panicking in the belief that his eyesight was gone forever and he clutched out in the direction of the voice, getting a lucky, frenzied grip on the fat man's lapels.

"I'm blinded, I'm blinded," he bleated in terror, clinging to the jacket as though the fat man was a leading ophthalmist and pulling him perilously close to the churned-up mess. The fat man had wanted to help, but not so badly as to risk spoiling his shoes and he tried to pull back. The youth clung to him all the harder, wailing constantly for help. The fat man regretted his rashness in getting himself involved and tried to extricate himself by pushing the youth in the chest and springing backwards. He succeeded to the sound of ripping cloth, parting with the youth and his left lapel simultaneously. The youth reached after him, lost his balance and fell to his knees in the goo.

Whatever idiot tricks the humans got up to bothered the dogs not at all. They ate on merrily, enjoying the un-accustomed sensation of bulging bellies, this unheard-of

(120)

opportunity to eat until they burst. Banjo tried to make the best of the opportunity but he had recently eaten two rolls and a hamburger so he was first to give up. He swallowed the last sausage it was possible to cram into his stomach, stood a moment panting and walked slowly away along the street, with the gathering crowd quickly moving away from his tomato-splashed sides. A police patrol was just drawing up to investigate the commotion reported in Vicar Lane.

The cause of the commotion, or at least part of the cause, walked slowly and unutterably happily down towards the rear of the market. It had been a long day, a rewarding day and the only way to end it was to find a sheltered place to sleep and let the huge meal digest in its own time.

Someone had left a barrow tipped up and leaning against a wall in a corner away from the street lights and noise, a perfect place to curl up under the axle and drift into soothing slumber. Banjo yawned a jaw-cracking yawn, flicked his tail to cover the tip of his nose and closed his eyes, at peace with the world and everything in it.

Chapter 7

(7)

Banjo slept well under the shelter of the cart, protected from the light dusting of frost which made the street phosphorescent, and did not wake until the owner of the cart loudly rattled the lock and chain. He was middle-aged and not unfriendly.

"Come on then, let's 'ave yer."

It was still very dark, no sign of the dawn, but the market people were about, raucous and jovial as they set up the 'flashes' of selected fruit and filled the stalls from delivery vans.

Banjo moved out from under the cart, stretched and yawned shudderingly, shook his body to fluff up his coat and felt ready to meet the day. There was something wrong with his fringe. Instead of hanging in separate strands like a bead curtain it was more like a piece of woven cloth with an inverted vee cut out for him to look through. He pawed at it once or twice but it was stiff and hard so he had another shake and went to see what was going on in the market.

Men in soiled white coats were carrying meat from covered vans into the row of butchers' shops and others were off-loading sacks of vegetables and boxes of fruit from flat-waggons. Everywhere was active. The meat was attractive but Banjo's belly was still overloaded—not that he would have refused a morsel or two if offered—so he had a general, casual mooch about, window-shopping for future reference.

The open-sided cafe was doing business with a crowd of

early starters gathered around, eating fragrant sandwiches and sipping tea, chatting, laughing, arguing. A man and two women were working behind the counter, one woman collecting dirty plates and scraping left-over food into a plastic bin. She was a young woman with a round, laughing face and when she saw Banjo weaving through the legs of the breakfasters, she threw him a piece of bacon sandwich.

"There y'are, love, you want your breakfast as well, don't you?"

Although he didn't need it, Banjo ate it as a matter of form; he was as partial as any human being to the taste of the bacon. The woman laughed again and dropped the white of a fried egg from which the yolk had been dipped. Banjo liked eggs, too, especially eggs fried in beef dripping like this one.

The man who was the proprietor poked the woman roughly on the shoulder, "Nark it! You'll 'ave every bloody dog there is 'angin' round if you start feedin' 'em."

A big man whose face was a road map of broken blood vessels and who proudly owned the loudest voice in the market thundered: "Give over, you're frightened you'll 'ave a bit less pig swill to sell, yer tight sod!"

The market men never wanted much of an excuse to have a joke and the coarse, vulgar remarks aimed at the cafe owner echoed down from the vaulted ceiling. He was likened to Ebenezer Scrooge, Uriah Heep, Adolf Hitler, Judge Jeffreys and, for some strange reason, Genghis Khan. But he was used to verbal batterings and the insults glanced off leaving him unabashed.

The young woman leaned over the counter to give Banjo a big wink, "Never mind him, love, call again when you're hungry."

Banjo didn't know what the wink signified but he knew he had made a friend. He carried on his morning constitutional along the top row of fruit stalls.

He turned left down the game row where the pheasants were being hung, the turkeys and chickens set out in lines on tiered shelves, down to the shellfish stall where Paul had bought whelks for him. Paul. His master's face came big

(126)

and clear into his head and he speeded up, trotting out through the bottom gate.

It was daylight now, or as light as a December day could be under an umbrella of thick, grey glowering clouds. People trudged along quickly to get out of the damp gloom into warm shops and offices. But Banjo trotted happily because he was going home and Paul would be waiting.

It was a fifteen-minute trot for Banjo, uphill nearly all the way and in that short space of time creatures more sensitive to temperature changes than he—well-wrapped humans—complained that it was getting colder by the second. Banjo's breath had been dispersing in a grey mist when he left the market but when he turned into the street it was a white trailing streamer as the cold gripped harder and started to turn the privet hedges white.

The narrow street was partly blocked by a large green van parked at Banjo's gate and two men were carrying the sideboard down the path. They were cursing the weather and walking carefully on the icy asphalt.

"Don't slip for Christ's sake, 'Arry."

"It's covered by insurance if we break it."

"Ah'm not bothered about that. You might pull me down as well. Hey up! There's a dog behind you. Gerraway, go on, piss off."

Banjo went round the men, passed the open front door and round the back, his entrance. The back door was closed but the need to see Paul was so great now he only barked and scratched once, then he broke the rules and ran round to the front, through the door and into his house.

But it was strange in the house. The living room was emptied of furniture, all that was left was the carpet, the curtains and the small litter bin standing forlornly in the middle of the floor, and the kitchen was not the same. All the cupboard doors were standing open, the cupboards empty, there was no tasty smell coming from the oven and the concrete floor of his kennel was as bare and clean as if it had just been swept. He could still pick up the scents of Paul, Madge and Denis but they were very faint and fading, old dying scents. Paul hadn't been in either of the

(127)

two rooms for a long time but Banjo was still sniffing about and looking into things when the two men came back.

"Ah don't like dogs," Harry said, standing uncertainly in the doorway, but his mate allayed his fears.

"No need to worry about this'n, it's quiet enough. It's just lookin' for summat. Let's get the carpet up, I'm ready for the caff."

Banjo stood in the kitchen doorway watching with head cocked as they ripped the carpet edges from the gripper rods and started to roll it up. They carried that away, came back for the underlay and then there was nothing of familiar friendliness left in the room but the curtains.

The forbidden upstairs. That was where Paul must be. Two years of total exclusion from that part of the house on the other side of the staircase door had made a barrier that was hard to break and he stood a moment looking up the bare wooden steps until the need for Paul overcame the discipline of strict instruction. When he started to climb, it was slowly, not unnervously at doing something he knew was wrong. He looked cautiously round the newel post onto the landing, expecting to hear Madge shout at him to get back down but all was still and quiet. Nothing moved and from what he could see of the rooms through the open doors they were as bare as the living room.

Cautiously he went onto the landing and into the first room. It was desolate, stripped of all sign of habitation, as lonely and lifeless as only an empty house can be but he was able to detect the faint scent of Denis and Madge. The second room he entered was not quite so large and he whined very softly as he made a circuit of the walls for Paul had been here to leave his evidence impregnated in the wallpaper and round the door handle. The smell of Paul was not stronger than that of his parents but it was everywhere in the room, distinctive and inescapable. Banjo lay down on the bare boards to wait for Paul to come home.

He could hear the men moving about below, the thud of their feet on the wood and the occasional creak of one of the boards, the click and rustle as the curtains were unhooked from the track and he heard one of them say:

(128)

"'as that dog gone?"

"Don't know. You take these out an' I'll 'ave a look round to make sure we 'aven't left owt."

He heard the man come up the stairs, heard him use the toilet and the cistern flush and then he was there in the doorway looking doubtful.

"Come on," said the man, "you can't stop 'ere, we've to lock up."

He walked round Banjo to touch his rump with a toe. "Come on, no messin' about, we've got work to do."

To the man's surprise and relief Banjo got up and went downstairs without any further prompting and, as the door to the living room was closed, out into the garden. As the man was locking the house, the woman next door came down her path dressed for the weather and huddled into her collar.

"D'you know whose this dog is?" he asked her across the hedge.

She glanced across disinterestedly. "It used to live there afore they went to Australia."

"Where's it live now?"

She did not even bother to look. "I don't know," she said and hurried down the street.

The removal man said, "Looks as though you're on your own, mate."

He swung up into the cab, the big engine roared and the van shuddered away into the greyness.

Banjo stood in the front garden looking at the house that had been his home, the curtainless windows like sightless eyes, a house without Paul, a dead house. Again he went to the back door but his bark was half-hearted and he didn't scratch, his limited intelligence at last accepting that Paul was not here and that he didn't know where to look for him. He ran down the path, jumped the closed gate and loped away with his breath trailing white in the tightening cold.

He couldn't plan his actions and now he knew he was homeless, unable to regulate his life with the old routine, he reverted completely to instinctive reflex living. He took his present direction of travel for no sound reason. He had

E (129)

to go somewhere, do something, so he just went and would do whatever was to be done when the need arose.

At that moment he lacked nothing, his stomach was still comfortably full from his gargantuan meal of the evening before. The weather was not thirst-inducing, his rough unkempt coat which was considered so unattractive by lovers of pedigree dogs was the perfect protection against the near-arctic climate. His reserves of strength built by two years of regular varied meals and the right kind of exercise, were intact and ready to be drawn upon and his newly gained, if unlooked for, freedom would have been the envy of many of his kind.

When he got to the main road he crossed it, neatly dodging the traffic, and went down through the warren of streets which was the path to the nearest park. Maybe there would be other dogs to run with.

There were no other dogs in the park, there was no animal life at all under the freezing skeletons of the trees. Not even any birds to scare. He had a good look, following the circuit he had made so many times before, and there were no boys playing football on the pitches. There was nobody and nothing for Banjo to be friendly with.

He left the park, going back up through the streets to the main road where there were people, but none of them wanted anything to do with him. He passed the end of his old street to pay a visit to the sports ground where he had always been taken for his early morning walk, but that was deserted as well so he kept on going.

He crossed the playing fields into the yard of the big factory and out through the main gates into more and more streets. It was not the first time he had been in the area but he had not visited it often and it held a certain amount of novelty with new smells to evaluate at the garden gates and at the feet of lamp posts.

He saw a Labrador trotting by the end of the street, the first dog he had seen that day and, eager for companionship, he took up pursuit. The Labrador was sturdy, well looked after and moving with a purpose, not roaming aimlessly like Banjo, and Banjo had to lengthen his stride to catch up.

(130)

The Labrador stopped and turned about when he heard Banjo closing on him. Banjo stopped too for the preliminary examination by nose. Satisfied Banjo was not an enemy to offer a threat, the black dog turned again to continue his original course. Banjo followed and the Labrador didn't seem to mind.

They came out of the narrow streets, crossed a wide busy road into a smaller road where the houses had privet hedges and large gardens. Soon they were three; a small fat mongrel with a short, white coat, black ears and a black patch on one shoulder, joined the procession. Shortly after that another two mongrels tagged on, both nearly as big as Banjo and one infinitely scruffier. As each newcomer arrived there was a halt in the march for the sniffing ceremony with every dog sniffing every other dog including those previously sniffed and then they were off again, all following the Labrador who seemed to be the only one who knew where they were going. Banjo didn't care where they were going. He wasn't hungry, he was among friends and that was sufficient.

Where they were going was to a garden gate and they were not the first to get there. There were already three dogs sitting in a rough semi-circle round the gate and the Labrador contingent made eight. They were all shapes and sizes, ranging from an emaciated sheepdog-type to the robust Labrador but they all took their seats to wait patiently.

Banjo didn't wonder why they waited, he didn't know the reason but it didn't trouble him and he was the only one not to sit—not until he had sniffed at the gate. The gate and posts carried a scent he had come across before, a tremendously exciting smell that he had never been allowed to follow and find its cause. Now he would find out. He sat between the Labrador and the sheepdog.

A milk float came rattling into the street, the driver grinning when he saw the waiting dogs, and when he made his first delivery he said to the housewife, "Mrs. Prior's bitch'll be all right if that lot cop her."

The woman laughed shrilly. "She will that, she'll think it's Christmas an' her birthday all rolled into one."

(131)

The milkman shook his head. "Beats me how they know. They must come from miles around."

The housewife said archly, "It's only like you men knowin' a good thing when you see one."

The milkman picked up the empties. "Yer, but we don't sit round in a circle to take turns."

She laughed again and closed her door. He had to go through the rank of dogs to deliver Mrs. Prior's milk and not a dog moved a muscle, he might not have existed. The eyes and attention of the dogs was immovably fixed on the house wherein dwelt the object of their collective desires. The Labrador's expression was nonchalantly bland, the small, black-eared mongrel's intent, the scrawny sheep-dog's avid, and Banjo was grinning.

The milkman rapped loudly on the door. "Any eggs, Mrs. Prior?"

The door opened, the merest crack. "Not today, love. Are them three dogs still there?"

"Three! There's eight!"

Mrs. Prior wailed. "Oh, an' my poor Penny'll be peein' herself if I don't take her out soon. Gerraway you mucky no-goods," she ended in a screech.

The milkman turned his head away so she couldn't see his grin. "Well, they're only lads. Let 'em have a bit o' fun, it'll do your Penny good."

Harsh and vitriolic were her comments on the state of the milkman's mind and she slammed the door in her frustration. The milkman made sure the gate was fastened and paused to address the dogs:

"I think you're wastin' your time sitting there in the cold, but I know what it's like when you fancy a bird. Anyway, good luck."

It took him twenty minutes to deliver to that street and when he looked back before turning the corner the dogs were exactly as he had left them.

Perhaps Banjo was the only completely inexperienced one at the game of waiting-at-the-gate and he had only the faintest inkling as to exactly why he was waiting, but he was first to weary of sitting in the cold. First he shook himself, then he had another sample of the scent on the

(132)

gate. This time it was not quite as strong but it had a much more positive effect on him and, still without knowing why he was doing it, he retreated a few paces, ran and cleared the gate with ease. The others, who knew what it was like to be hit or kicked by the jealous owners of bitches, remained where they were.

The smell was much stronger around the side door of the house but the door was closed and offered no promise or hope. But from the back of the house floated another smell, not as intriguing, but possibly with a more available source. The smell of cooking food. He still wasn't hungry but he would never be guilty of passing up a chance to eat.

It was coming, the fragrant steam, from the partly open kitchen window and carried with it the evidence that there was meat as well as vegetables simmering in the pan and it was just as he was lifting his head to catch the full flavour of the smell that Mrs. Prior decided in desperation that she would have to put her plan, which was the only way of allowing her Penny to make a much-needed toilet, into operation.

Preferring bitches to dogs, she had years ago taken the necessary precaution of making her garden escape-proof. The wire netting running along inside the privet hedges not only stopped her beloved Penny from flaunting herself, at the wrong times, but also barred the entry of any amorous suitors. The one vulnerable point was the gate. And that would not be vulnerable when she stood over it with the sweeping brush she was prepared to brandish.

When Penny was showing signs that to deprive her of toilet facilities any longer would be disastrous, Mrs. Prior picked up her brush, took a deep breath and said to the apple of her eye, who was an apricot miniature poodle, "Now you stay there a minute, love, till I shout," as though she was talking to her favourite grandchild. Penny obe-diently stayed in the kitchen as her mistress flung open the door and rushed up the path to the gate as quickly as her sixty-year-old legs would carry her. The dogs were there, seven not eight as the milkman had said, and she rested the brush on the top of the gate.

Standing sideways and trying to watch the dogs and the

door she shouted, "Come on, Penny, be quick, It's bloody cold out here." Penny leapt from the door and started to run to Mrs. Prior. Mrs. Prior flapped her free hand. "No, love, no. Go back, go on!"

The strategy was new to Penny but she got the idea she was not wanted at the gate and the need to relieve herself was reaching gigantic proportions. She turned and raced out of sight around the corner of the house. Mrs. Prior turned her full attention to the waiting dogs—all of which had perked up remarkably with the brief appearance of Penny—and there was something very smug and satisfied about the way she brandished her brush over the top of the gate. She had outwitted them.

Several minutes went by, and Mrs. Prior got cold and very impatient, estimating Penny had had at least twice as long as she needed to carry out her natural functions. She shouted, "Penny! Penny! Come on, love, I'm freezing."

No lovingly obedient Penny bounded round the corner at the call of her mistress and her mistress felt the first twinge of anxiety. It was not like her Penny to ignore a command.

"Penny! Penny!"

When she looked at the dogs again, they had inched their way a little closer to the gate and she jabbed at them with the brush. "Gerraway you dirty beasts. Go, go on!"

The grinning dogs grinned, the frowning dogs frowned and the Labrador stayed expressionless, but showed he intended to be the first to ravish Penny in the set of his shoulders and the tenseness of his fine muscles.

"*Penny!*"

Mrs. Prior's voice was scratchy with apprehension when the Poodle didn't appear. She had been behind the house ten minutes now, ample time for anything. There must be something wrong. Mrs. Prior leaned over the gate and made a scything sweep with the brush to scatter the dogs but they didn't scatter far, a few paces back. Taking what she could of the slight advantage she ran down the path and as she reached the corner of the house the virile body of the Labrador sailed majestically over the gate. The scruffy mongrel was next, then the Sheepdog—with

(134)

something of a scramble—then two together like Grand National runners. Last was the small black and white dog and the gate was too high for him, time and again he scurried up on his short legs, made a valiant leap only to hit the gate half way up and rebound back onto the pavement.

The stream of dogs raced down the path and skidded round a horrified Mrs. Prior who was standing transfixed, one hand on the wall for support. Standing placidly in the frost-rimmed grass, coupled firmly rear to rear, were her beloved Penny and a grey dog with a matted, filthy coat. The seven visiting dogs started to make a thorough canine examination of the lovers; and Banjo grinned up at Mrs. Prior.

Her anger was slow to overcome her righteous mortification. It started in her motherly breast, spread upwards to her head and reddened her face, outwards to her limbs and made them shake.

In the time it took her to go and collect the brush from where she had dropped it at the side door, nature had run its full course. Banjo was stretching and shaking himself and the grateful Labrador was in the act of mounting the amenable Penny. Gasping breathlessly, Mrs. Prior, holding the brush in the tradition of the Infantry like a rifle and bayonet, charged across the grass to knock the Labrador off balance. As he fell sideways, the sheepdog obligingly moved in to take his place and when he was buffeted away the Labrador was back to beat the scruffy dog to the target.

"Don't just stand there," Mrs. Prior screamed at Penny, whose morals she was beginning to suspect, "get inside!" She continued unsuccessfully the battle of warding off the dogs until she realised the only permanent way was to remove the temptress. For the fourth time she drove off the persistent Labrador, dropped the brush, scooped Penny up to her bosom and ran into the house slamming the door in the trailing Labrador's face. The dogs then formed their semi-circle round the side door and settled down to wait again. Except Banjo. Having thoroughly enjoyed his first mating he was now feeling the pangs of hunger and decided it was time to start foraging. He jumped the gate

(135)

and started back in the direction from which he had come when the snow started.

There was no breeze at all and the snow came down straight and silent and soft, the big flakes lying on the frozen ground, not melting, forming first an erratic pattern which gradually filled in to quickly obscure the pavements and roofs. The traffic-churned roads were black and wet but Banjo trotted along happily on the crunching white carpet, heading for the place of certain food, the market.

The falling flakes intensified making visibility bad for pedestrians, almost impossible for motorists but Banjo moved at his normal trot, knowing exactly where he was going.

He was in luck again. A small café at the bottom of the market opened early and closed early and as Banjo passed through the gates the cook was in the act of carrying out a bin of left-overs for collection by the swill men. The cook left the lidless bin against the wall inside the gate and the smell of the wasted food was as good as a homing device. It was not as high as a dustbin and with a little neck stretching Banjo could reach the top layer which was made up mostly of bacon rind and partly eaten pieces of breadcake.

For the second time in his life he was able to eat his capacious fill and he took full advantage, uncovering all kinds of titbits as he nosed the bread aside. Beneath the bread were the plate scrapings from lunchtime, shreds of beef and pork, pieces of sausage, roast potatoes, chips, mash, suet pudding with jam, all none the less delicious because they were cold, leathery, and in some cases fat enshrouded. The bread and bacon rind he left for the pigs, burying his muzzle in congealed gravy and custard, both nicely spiced with the flavour of H.P. sauce. If the day's long walk aided by the marital exercise had not made him ravenous, the mouth-watering contents of the swill bin would have done, and he gluttonously gulped down mouthful after mouthful, comforted by the sensation of his filling stomach.

But the greatest gourmands have a limit and Banjo had his, extensive though it was. He reached it regretfully, the

(136)

bin still holding an awful lot of tasty morsels, walked heavily into a dark corner by the gate stanchions, curled up and went to sleep. The free life was good and rewarding for a dog who knew his way around and as he slept he twitched in his dreams of the Poodle bitch, food and the freedom to roam as he willed. He sighed and sank into the deep, deep sleep of the contented.

His after-lunch nap was broken by the toe of a boot poked unrelentingly into his ribs. A tall man wearing a raincoat and a flat cap was standing over him.

"Come on," said the man, "let's 'ave yer. I'm waitin' to lock up." He rattled a large bunch of keys as if to bear out his statement.

Banjo had a stretch, a yawn and a shake, scattering the melted snow from his back and the man growled, "Hey up, then! I'll be wet enough afore I get 'ome."

There was only the staff in the market now and the sounds they made as they checked for security were loud in the emptiness. The man impatiently poked at Banjo again, "Go on, gerrout."

His meaning was obvious and Banjo went. It was very dark but the big drifting flakes reflected the street lights brilliantly, giving a cold beauty to the narrow street. On the paths and roads the snow had been trampled away but now the people and cars were all gone a white sheet was quickly covering the dirty slush. The gates clanged behind him as he set off aimlessly up the street with nowhere to go but everywhere to go, free to the whims of his fancy.

His fancy took him on a tour of the shopping centre where the lighted windows of the closed shops made the streets as bright as day but where there was nothing to hold his attention, so he took a road away from the centre, a road he didn't know very well. The farther he got from the centre the less trampled was the snow and in some places he ploughed belly deep. But he didn't mind, the elements meant little to him, the secure ties of a warm fireplace were behind him, he had exchanged the comforts provided by people for the liberty of emancipation.

The road was long and steadily uphill and the few people he saw were hurrying timidly on the precarious footing, eager to get inside wherever they were going and the few drivers who had braved the weather ground slowly along in low gear.

It was a fairly good road liberally spaced with the most interesting establishments of all, food shops. There were fish and chip shops, fried chicken shops, Chinese take-aways and cafés. At each one he stopped for a smell of the gusts of warm air gushing from hastily opened and closed doors but his inspections were purely academic: his belly was still weighty from the swill bin. He did not pause long anywhere but kept going steadily up the road.

The built-up area melted away after the last cluster of shops and there was a wide expanse of grass on either side of the road, the street lights were fewer and he knew that he had been here before a long time ago. On his right the unbroken plain of white sparkled under the lights and faded into the darkness of the distance. The newness of the snow blanket was inviting. He turned off the road to romp and leap and cut a ragged scar in the snow, he ran out and away from the lights behind him until more lights showed in a blur through the fog-thick falling snow. It was another road to follow and he did know this one, it led down a curving hill to a big park with two lakes.

The lights ended completely at the bottom of the hill and before him the park was so dark even the falling snow was invisible. It kept on falling, though, softly and wetly onto his muzzle, silently clinging to his insulated coat until he looked like a ghost dog, a white head and body moving in the night.

He found nothing in the park, no people, no dogs, no ducks, just trees and snow and the black cold lakes. Finally he wearied of questing for he knew not what and started to look for a place to sleep and found it at the top of a little hill. It was a small round building with no door, made of wood and glass with a bench seat running round the outside. There was a similar seat running round the inside, just at the right height for Banjo to lie under. There was no heating but the air was still and with the snow shaken off his back it was quite warm enough for him. He curled

(138)

up in the blackness under the bench and within minutes he was dreaming.

Banjo slept late, wakened only by the growing light and the soft moan of the wind through the bare branches of the trees and the rhythmic dripping of water. The early winter snow had already started to thaw, the warm wind turning the park from a winter playground into a damp place of rivulets and runnels and constant dripping. His left side was dry, his right side on which he had slept was still damp and the concrete was marked with the water from his body. He had his stretch and yawn and shake and went out into the wet world.

Except for the birds, the park was still devoid of any sign of life so with nothing to hold his interest he set off south for the area he liked best, the city centre with its providential market.

Back down the long road, now with only the newsagents open, with the long impatient bus queues and the vehicles churning the snow to filthy water. The firm, dry snow in the darkness was better. It was good to go to new or different places but it was better to be going to his own place in that wonderland of smells and surprise meals, not that he was hungry yet. He had reached a large busy crossroads before he thought of the Poodle bitch and instead of going straight ahead with the people taking advantage of the traffic lights, he turned left up the hill, knowing this was the way to where the Poodle lived.

He found the house easily and he was the first one there. He followed the routine which he had learned the day before from the more experienced dogs; he waited at the gate but because of the slushy pavement he stood instead of sitting. The snow had almost blotted out the smell on the gate but it was detectable.

He waited there a long time in the wet. He had no plan of action and, if his desires were to be fulfilled, it would need, as yesterday, a fortuitous chain of events. But today there was no stew cooking to draw him to the rear of the house, no gang of dogs to draw Mrs. Prior to the gate, only Banjo and the disappearing snow.

He reared up and put his feet on the top bar of the gate

to view the terrain, hoping that the bitch might trot into sight. But it was not a bitch—a female, but not canine—who came charging from the house waving her sweeping brush like a crusader with a battle axe. Mrs. Prior had seen him from the window, the despoiler of her adorable Penny, and although Banjo had no reasoning power he got the general idea that he was not exactly welcome.

When Mrs. Prior lashed down at his head he sprang lithely back into the road and Mrs. Prior was minus one sweeping brush when the shaft cracked down onto the top bar—where Banjo's skull should have been—and snapped off below the head. She leaned over the gate and waved her shaft like a crusader who had changed weapons.

"Gerraway, you dirty swine. Go on, gerraway!"

Banjo was out of range of the shaft and he would never be vanquished by threats. He stood in the middle of the road, his lower half soaked and filthy-looking, his top half matted and tangled, his fringe still bearing traces of the tomato sauce. The thought of such a disreputable-looking fleabag siring the offspring of the earth's most lovable bitch drove Mrs. Prior into a blind rage. She opened the gate and advanced on Banjo at the same time as the milk float clanked and squelched into the street.

The dripping, oozing world had not dampened the milkman's sense of fun or his appreciation of the ridiculous. At the sight of the sixty-year-old woman moving at the backing dog with the footwork of a fencer, her balance ever in peril on the treacherous surface, he shouted:

"Thrust, Parry, Lunge. That's it, Mrs. Prior, run the mucky bugger through."

Word of Penny's fall from grace had raced around the street as though Mrs. Prior herself had been caught behaving shamefully in her back garden and the fact that the story had reached the ears of the raucous-voiced milkman did not lessen her chagrin. She doubled her efforts to get in a telling blow at the perpetrator, who now saw that with the woman in the middle of the street the way to the bitch was clear.

With his claws to give him the advantage of a firm grip he raced around Mrs. Prior, carefully keeping out of range,

(140)

and up the path to the back door. The milkman had braked his float to watch the comedy.

"Go on, lad," he encouraged, but not wanting to seem biased or partial, added, "After 'im, Mrs. Prior, give 'im some stick."

Mrs. Prior, all but foaming at the mouth, was literally the cause of her own downfall; she tried to turn too quickly and sat with a thump in the slush. Her substantially padded behind saved her from real injury and she howled out of anguished frustration more than physical hurt. She struggled hard to get to her feet but the soles of her shoes skidded from under her and she looked rather like an athlete performing a leg strengthening exercise.

"Steady on, love," the milkman called, "I'm comin'."

"Spoilsport," one watching woman grinned from her bedroom window, "let the dog 'ave 'is day."

The milkman winked and set out to the rescue, teetering down the middle of the street with a false show of haste. He had no intention of seriously trying to save Penny from her fate.

"O.K., mate, I'm with you," he said softly when he saw Banjo sniffing at the side door of the house. The retelling of this morning's events would earn him unlimited cups of tea right into the far distant future.

"Come on!" Mrs. Prior blared at him. "It's goin' to be too late."

"I know what you mean but he can't do any more damage than he did yesterday, can he?" He continued his laboured progress.

When Mrs. Prior had seen Banjo at the gate her only thought had been to punish him for his crime and drive him away forever and she had pulled the door behind her but had not checked that the latch had clicked home. The latch had not gone home, leaving a half-inch gap from the door edge to the stop-lath. Through the gap came the seasonal smell of the bitch who was standing the other side of the door listening to the raised voices in the street. As Banjo took huge inhalations of the greatest drawing card in the canine world the bitch caught his scent and whined appealingly. He pushed at the door, opening

(141)

it a foot or so, wide enough for Penny to come out to him.

Unlike peacocks, Banjo didn't find it necessary to go through a long and complicated routine of preening and showing himself off before getting down to the mating act, and Penny didn't expect it for dogs are very basic and uncomplicated in their mental make-up, not given to extraneous frivolities.

Clinging to the arm of the milkman, Mrs. Prior had now got herself upright just in time to watch the ugly, filthy mongrel start the act of copulation right outside her door. Horrified, outraged, pop-eyed and speechless she tried to run forward and was saved from another fall by the grip of the milkman.

"Steady, love, steady. You'll do no good if you break your leg."

Clinging together like lost waifs they started down the slippery path at a pace dictated by the milkman designed to make sure they were going to be too late. Every time Mrs. Prior tried to dart forward he would feign a skid and hold her back.

"Whoops, go careful, love."

The woman who was watching from her bedroom window shouted to her neighbour, "Quick, Doris, 'ave a look at this. It's funnier than Benny 'ill."

More faces appeared at windows and doors opened as Banjo's audience built up. And Banjo, in Mrs. Prior's opinion, had the effrontery to grin at her over Penny's head as he got on with his task.

The milkman observed conversationally. "He doesn't stick fast, that dog, does he? Your Penny's a good bit smaller than 'im, but 'e's managing all right."

Perhaps it was a good thing Mrs. Prior's ire was still rendering her incapable of speech.

The milkman's strategy had worked. Banjo and Penny were locked rear to rear again before Mrs. Prior got her hands on him and if Penny had not conceived the previous day she certainly would have done now. However, the inevitable did not detract from Mrs. Prior's thirst for vengeance and she regretted having left the brush handle in the street.

"You ... You ..." she choked at Banjo, "I'll kill you!"

"Nay," the milkman reasoned, "it's too late now an' 'e was only doin' what comes naturally, *and* your Penny must be as bad. Don't blame the men all the time."

That made sense and if Mrs. Prior's rage was not to any degree cooled, the words at least made her turn some of it onto Penny.

"You dirty little cow," she hissed.

The tableau in the garden held until Penny released Banjo and, no longer interested in the house or its occupants, Banjo widely skirted round the enraged woman, stopped in the gateway to shake and loped off up the street, hearing Mrs. Prior taking Penny to task and the laughter of the watching women.

Chapter 8

(8)

By the middle of the afternoon only the last traces of the snow remained in the gutters in shrinking, dirty heaps and in the city centre there was no trace at all. The ground was black and wet but the continuing wind was drying that up, too. Youngsters despaired of seeing a white Christmas and the elderly were cheered by the mildness of the weather. It all made no difference to Banjo—rain, snow, heat, wind—he got on with the business of living the unfettered life and was unmolested.

For two weeks he seldom suffered undue hunger pangs, always finding a fresh source of food when the regular ones were for some reason unavailable to him. He was a little nonplussed on the days, Sundays, when the gates of the market were not opened at all, cutting him off from breakfast by courtesy of the kindly woman at the open-sided cafe, and dinner at the swill bins. He had tracked down the location of several swill bins and hidey holes where the confectioners dumped stale cakes and buns for collection by the refuse men. To him the market was one big kitchen. But the Sundays kept him on his mettle, stopped him from becoming too complacent and lazy.

On these non-market days he had to go searching if he wanted to eat and his most useful weapon in the hunt, his nose, never let him down, guiding him into five back alleys where restaurants and cafes kept their swill bins. These places were filed away in his memory to be held on standby, his ace in the hole for lean times. Four of the five, at least. Had he been capable he would have wished the removal of the fifth from the face of the earth. Actually this fifth was the first one he discovered.

It was his second Sunday of emancipation, one week after the capsizing of the hot-dog stand, and he had hung around the market all day waiting for someone to open the gates. In the evening he was lying by the top gates in the shadow cast by the street lights when he saw the youth push the hot-dog stand along the road from wherever it was garaged and into the side street to start work. In a little while the breeze carried the scent of frying. As it was long after Banjo's regular feeding time, his stomach rolled and his mouth filled with saliva, overcoming his caution, but he did make his approach with diffidence.

He slunk into the side street close to the wall, on the opposite side from the youth and his stand, and took up a position of observation in the dark shop doorway to drink in the aroma. The youth didn't see him immediately. Banjo watched, waited and sniffed hungrily.

There came a time when the effect of the smells on Banjo's taste buds and clawing stomach was so powerful that he moved out of the doorway into the bright yellow light of the pavement, to sit with his eyes switching from the youth's face to the smell-producing stand and its contents. The youth saw him then, but had, apparently, decided he was beneath consideration and turned back to the indolent stirring of the onions. If this behaviour was not precisely encouraging, neither was it off-putting and Banjo moved closer, keeping however a respectful distance and sitting in the middle of the street, his rapt gaze on the sallow face of the youth. A person of a forgiving nature might have read adulation into Banjo's grinning expression, might have let bygones be bygones and proffered an olive branch in the shape of a bread roll, but the youth was of sterner stuff. He stirred his onions with his right hand, hovering his left over the stick lying ready on the shelf.

Each time the youth served one of his occasional customers Banjo became a little bolder, stole a little closer as the youth's back was to him. The youth didn't seem to mind and now Banjo could see the dripping sausages and burgers as they were placed in the split rolls and smothered

(148)

with onions and tomato sauce. The tomato sauce should have, by thought association, brought to the fore the unpleasant experience seven days earlier but if it suggested danger to him the exciting closeness of the food drove it from his head. One must be a bit adventurous.

Banjo ventured another forward shuffle which took him exactly where the vengeful youth wanted him, within the diameter of the distance from his shoulder to the end of the stick when swung at arm's length.

"Fifteen pence," the youth said as he handed over a hot sandwich and with a fairly fluid movement pocketed the cash, snatched up the club-like stick and swung it overhead in the manner of a fast bowler. In dealing with dogs, fortune was not with him. On its way to the top of the arc the stick neatly struck the hot-dog from the fingers of the astonished customer hurling it in a high parabola over Banjo's head with sausage, onions and bread parting company in flight and no boxer ever telegraphed a punch more than the youth did his attempt to brain Banjo. Banjo had turned to retrieve the food and was out of reach before the stick started its downward swing. Had the youth left it at that, all would have been well—discounting the fact that he was out of pocket by the cost of one hot-dog—but such was his desire to maim Banjo that he overreached, jarred the shaft of the cart and sent the piled-up rolls cascading down into the street. He roared madly at this second catastrophe, ignored the demands of the customer for a replacement and rushed after Banjo waving his stick intent on murder.

To elude the apoplectic youth was no trouble at all to Banjo and he had plenty of time to make a slight detour to pick up the battered sausage from the far pavement, gulp it down, snatch the dirty roll and carry it off to be eaten later. The infuriated seller of hot-dogs hurled his stick across the widening gap in a last attempt to extract some kind of retribution but he was wider of the mark when using the stick as an assegai than as a knobkerrie. With the danger removed, Banjo impertinently stopped to devour his stolen roll twenty yards from the fuming youth, who returned to his customers to give a lengthy and detailed

(149)

description of what he would do to that dog next time it came to cause havoc in his life.

The sausage and roll were very good, but were no more than an appetiser after a fast of more than twenty-four hours so Banjo set off on a determined, if aimless, search for food.

To the canine sense of smell, estimated by a Swedish expert to be a thousand times more sensitive than man's, the air in the city centre with its cafés and restaurants always carried evidence that food was not far away. Banjo raised his head, sniffed at the slight breeze and took off at a fast trot following the airborne trail, his pace increasing with the intensifying of the scent.

There were three cafés all in a cluster, all open for business, but all inaccessible to him. Through the windows he could see the diners putting food into their mouths and his own filled with saliva, the overspill pouring from his lips in a thin stream. He could not get at the food but its nearness, the sight of it, held him as firm as any lead or rope. Back and forth past the three windows he went, stimulating the saliva glands and aggravating the increasing stomach contractions. Each time someone entered or left one of the cafés, he ran to the door hopefully but no one let him in or gave him anything to eat.

For an hour or more he patrolled this beat in a state of gastronomic torture and was at the topmost cafe when he saw a man eating something from a paper on the other side of the road. His attention switched from the succulent but unobtainable dishes in the cafés to the probably acquirable something in the paper and he ran across the road.

The man appeared not to notice him as he kept pace, eyes never leaving the hand that was travelling from paper to mouth and back again, and when the man—who was not *exactly* staggering—screwed up the paper and tossed it into the gutter Banjo dived after it to paw and smell but the predominant smell was of strong vinegar without the accompaniment of fish or chips. Whatever the vinegar had been used to dress was gone now, the paper was empty and Banjo still had nothing to eat.

It was then the breeze strengthened and gusted another

(150)

scent down the road, a strange unknown scent, but indubitably connected with food. Banjo ran towards the scent.

He passed the end of a narrow street that had the illuminated windows of cafés and turned into an even narrower one running parallel, an alley of small gateless yards and in one of the yards the trail ended. From a lidless dustbin the thick odour was rising to fill the yard with an invisible pungent cloud. Banjo practically attacked the dustbin for, now he was close, he picked up the secondary smell of meat.

He reared up to put his paws on the rim of the bin and reach inside only to find the food was at the bottom. Eagerly he strained to get his head down, he fought and scrabbled his hind legs until the inevitable occurred and the bin tipped over; then it was easy. He walked into the bin, each rocking step making a loud clanging rattle, and snatched greedily at the meat. It was plate scrapings, hefty cubes of meat mixed with vegetables ... and something else. For the first split second he was conscious only of his fangs sinking into the glorious chunks, but in the next second, the 'something else' attacked him. It burned deep into his tongue, scorched the roof of his mouth, seared his lips and inflamed his gums. He sprang backwards out of that bin as though propelled by gun powder, sucked in a mouthful of air which only seemed to increase the agony as if there were an actual fire burning. Never in his life had he known such intense unremitting pain and he shook his head wildly, madly trying to dislodge the soft meat skewered on his teeth but it clung stubbornly, driving the terrific heat deeper into his palate and the very roots of his tongue. Round the yard he blundered blindly, his eyes brimming with tears, shaking and tossing his head, trying to get rid of the torment but it was no good; whatever had been on the meat had coated his mouth and it clung there grimly, burning, burning.

Water! He had to have water and there was none in the yard or the street; the cold wet slush had all drained away into the sewers and the only water he knew was away at the bottom end of the market where the tap dripped. He

(151)

started to run, not his casual lope or brisk trot, a full-stretch gallop down the alley and a wide swinging turn into the road at the bottom. A car braked and hooted, missed him by a yard and he actually bumped into the side of a crawling bus but cars, buses, people didn't matter. Water mattered and he had to get it.

He careered blindly over the cross roads but it was Sunday evening and the traffic was light; he turned down the side of the market at the same mad pace, running faster than ever, even accelerating a little as he got closer to the water.

One small point in his favour was that worn tap washers do not improve with use; the washer in this tap was leaking at a faster rate than previously and he put up his mouth to catch every globule of the dribble. It was slowly dispensed but the cold soothing balm brought magical relief from the misery.

He stayed at the tap a long time until his mouth had cooled down to a bearable temperature. His gums, tongue and lips still tingled, a slight discomfort that was nothing compared to what he had suffered. It was his misfortune that the distinctive smell of curry travels far, that he had found the rear of an Indian restaurant and that he had tried to eat the remains of that most fiery of all dishes, Vindaloo. But the misadventure had not been entirely without profit for he had learned that dustbins are kept in other places as well as markets, always where it is dark and quiet, where a dog can feed in peace.

In his third week of being a stray there was a noticeable difference about his favourite haunt, the city centre. There were more people in the streets bustling and jostling and loaded with packages and parcels. The market was almost impossible, thronged from end to end and side to side, so densely packed with shoppers it became a work of art for a dog to make his way to the swill bins without being trodden on. Banjo didn't like this influx. He didn't mind people—he liked them—but there is a limit to how many can squeeze into a market, however large that market may be, and sometimes it seemed they would have to start walking on top of one another.

(152)

As there was no pleasure in being buffeted and squashed, he usually ate at the back of his cafés and the thick crowds in all the streets drove him to going afield more often. He crossed the river into the industrial district, going far out to where the fields started, he went west a long way often finding dogs to play with in the park-like ground of the ruined abbey, he went north to the park with two lakes and east to the places Paul had taken him.

He now accepted the fact that Paul was unobtainable and his ex-master came less and less into his thoughts as the yearning diminished. He was fatalistic, accepting what is and not despairing over what could be.

As the crowds built up he used the city centre only for eating and sleeping, eating at night after making a day-long trek and sleeping close to wherever he had found food. He was happy to roam and sleep or eat as he willed or, rather, as his instinct dictated, and no one bothered him. He was not the only dog to go into the market unaccompanied and the people who saw him regularly assumed he had a home somewhere close.

On the morning of the busiest day he had ever seen, when the pavements were crowded like the stands of a football ground, he woke in an alley behind one of his cafés. He had slept longer than he usually did—because an unsuccessful trek after a bitch scent had kept him up late—although it was early by the standards of the shoppers, and when he came out of the alley the streets were already beginning to fill. In the time it took him to go to the bottom of the market for a drink, more buses had disgorged more shoppers and the market was doing a far bigger trade than on any Saturday afternoon, so Banjo turned his back on it all and went to the north. He had taken a great liking to the park with two lakes.

It was biting cold: eaves, gutters and rainwater pipes were festooned with icicles and sheet ice, exhaled breath was white smoke and every indrawn breath chilled the nostrils. The sun was a pale yellow ball shining weakly through the grey overcast sky and youngsters hoped again for a white Christmas whilst the greybeards told them it was far too cold. Maybe if it got warmer ... It got colder,

(153)

but it snowed; fine breeze-flung pellets nearly as hard as hail forming drifts in the gutters and corners.

People huddled, shivered and complained but Banjo's pace was jaunty, his large evening meal still generating heat and energy. Into the wind he trotted, body protected by the coarse, matted coat, eyes by the filthy fringe, his long, thin legs working easily. Nobody—with the exception of Paul Holmes—would ever defend uncomplimentary statements about Banjo's looks for he was an ugly dog by any measure and now he was homeless, the dirt his shaggy hair was accumulating did nothing to enhance him. But in the bitter English winter there was something graceful in the way he moved with an utter lack of concern for the conditions. He was a dog without a care, perfectly happy to go on fending for himself, needing no one.

The road leading down to the biggest and first of his lakes was lined on one side with houses, some new, some large and old but all with extensive gardens, and some with dogs. It was his custom to have a barking match with these house dwellers as he passed. They would rush up to the gate and snap furiously at him and he would pause to give a short reply.

The first was a beautiful Springer Spaniel, a bitch who always barked loudly but never with real menace. The second was a Labrador, black as the night and with the typical kindly nature of the breed who seemed to bark only not to be left out. The noisiest of them all, and the most playful, was an off-white Afghan Hound whose barking was surely nothing but an invitation for Banjo to jump the high fence and have a game.

The fourth was a different type of dog altogether, a brindle Staffordshire Bull Terrier, not nearly as big as Banjo, short and squat with bowed legs and a pugnacious face, one of a breed into which fearless fighting qualities had been bred. When this one barked it was in earnest, issuing a challenge to come and do battle, to fight to the death or until his adversary could elude his jaws and escape.

This Staffordshire, who bore the unsuitable name of Teddy, had an idolising and foolish master who enjoyed regaling his friends with exaggerated stories of Teddy's battling prowess; a master who thought that any dog worthy of the name should be a killer by instinct and that of all the breeds, he had chosen the most deadly to guard his possessions. The way he had mollycoddled, petted and generally spoiled Teddy had made him a possessive, jealous animal with a short temper.

He had been sitting eating a bone in the driveway when the snow had started, so had left the bone and gone into the warm shelter of the lounge from which window he liked to watch the world when the weather was inclement. There he was sitting, on an expensive, claw-marked table, when he heard the dogs up the street bidding Banjo good morning. He stiffened, sat and watched. His master, who was in the room, strolled to the window to see what had set Teddy on edge.

The front garden wall was four feet high, too high for Teddy to jump with his short legs and bulky body and when Banjo appeared at the gate to look in on the Staffordshire, the man in the window put a hand on his dog's head.

"Steady, Teddy."

Teddy stiffened up more, a low growl vibrating his whole body.

Banjo had looked through the bars of the gate ready to give voice and the first thing he saw was the bone. It was a knuckle bone, white and bare of meat, a gnawing bone of no food value. Banjo loved the pleasure of a contented chew and there was no one in sight, the bone holding his attention to the exclusion of the watchers in the window. The garden wall that was too high for Teddy was no barrier at all to Banjo; he did not even need to take a run, he was up and over with his surprising agility.

Teddy's master grinned and snapped his finger. "Come on, Ted, you can have a bit of fun."

They ran through the lounge and up the corridor to the front door, the squat, thick, fighting dog with jaws almost as strong as his cousin the Bulldog getting there first and waiting agitatedly for his laggard master.

As Banjo picked up the bone the door opened, releasing the belligerent Teddy as though he had been fired from a

(155)

catapult. He came flying across the corner of the garden with lips drawn back and murder in his eyes for the dog who had not only dared to come onto his property but had the temerity to steal his bone.

Banjo had the bone in his mouth and humans are not the only animals to consider that possession is nine-tenths of the law. He turned quickly to make his run to the wall and he nearly got there. He was faster than the Staffordshire but the angry dog had the advantage of a flying start and Banjo's acceleration was not quite enough to get him out of reach. Teddy hit him as he was bunching for the take-off and together they crashed into the wall. Teddy's ancestors, bred and trained to fight bulls, would have very quickly turned Banjo into a corpse with the inescapable throat hold, but Teddy had not been trained to do this by his doting master and so he bit into the nearest thing available, Banjo's ear.

Banjo yelped sharply with the stinging pain, tried to get his teeth into Teddy, Teddy bit down harder and Banjo screamed, jerked away madly, screamed again as the gristle and sinews tore. He jumped back blindly, as much in shocked surprise as pain, gave his head a shake and scattered blood drops into the settling snow.

Teddy's master was not actually a cruel man though he didn't mind his dog handing out the odd nip now and then and when he saw the red stream pouring from Banjo's severed ear he shouted:

"That'll do, Teddy, come on, you've won."

He would have had more success ordering the wind to stop driving the snow pellets into his face. Teddy dropped the piece of ear and lunged forward again. Banjo was overwhelmed with a boiling hatred for the stocky dog and sprang to meet him. They were both clear of the ground when they collided. Snarling horrifically, they fell rolling and squirming, snapping, seeking to inflict the utmost injuries.

Banjo didn't fight like Teddy who was striving for a death grip at the throat, he bit quickly and often, slashing open Teddy's cheek and going even wilder at the taste of the hot blood. Another clash of teeth and the blood spouted from Teddy's upper lip, but nothing short of death would put him off his desire to get at Banjo's windpipe.

The hair-raising noise of the fight brought a woman running out into the next garden. She looked over the hedge, saw the flying blood.

"Stop 'em," she shouted angrily at Teddy's master, "don't just stand there."

Like Doctor Frankenstein, Teddy's master had created something he could not control and he was wishing heartily that he had kept Teddy indoors. The woman jolted him into action and not a moment too soon. Teddy got a grip on Banjo's throat, and the master knew what that meant. He turned and ran for the garden shed.

Banjo struggled like a fish on a hook, twisting, wriggling, clawing frantically at Teddy's body with his paws but the jaws buried in the hair of his neck tightened, tightened, squeezing his windpipe until he had to suck with every ounce of strength to draw in air. And all the time, the blood pumped from the jagged edge of what remained of his ear.

His matted coat was his salvation, the thick, rug-like growth round his neck gave Teddy more to bite through, stopping him from fully closing the gullet. This allowed Banjo to take in the vital air until Teddy's master ran back from the shed carrying a long-handled rake.

He knew his dog, was aware that no amount of beating or pleading would make him let go and when he forced the end of the handle into Teddy's jaws Banjo's struggles were getting weaker. Taking a good hold on Teddy's collar he prised sideways with the rake, straining to give Banjo enough clearance to pull away, bending the handle dangerously close to breaking point before Teddy's jaws slowly started to open.

The relief was immediate. Banjo lay on his side in the driving snow wheezing, dragging in the beautiful cold air as Teddy was hauled, struggling to get back to the fight, into the garden shed. In one quick movement his master slung him deep into the shed and slammed the door whereupon the thwarted dog set up a racket of barking, growling, snarling and crashing as he hurled himself time and again at the door.

(157)

Banjo was on his feet, pawing at his bleeding ear and shaking his head, flinging the blood about the garden. Now his lungs were full of oxygen again, he felt better and there was only the sting of his ear to bother him—and *that* was not really bad, annoying more than anything.

The woman was still watching across the hedge. She said as her neighbour came back from the shed, "You ought to do something about that poor dog's ear. It might bleed to death."

With the danger to Banjo's life removed, Teddy's master was his braggardly self. He laughed. "Teach him to keep off where he doesn't belong." He laughed louder, "And not to pinch bones—not my Teddy's bones, anyway. He'll be all right and I want him out of here so's I can ring the vet for Teddy, he'll need a stitch or two in his lip." He opened the gate wide, jerked his head at Banjo, "Come on, away you go."

There was no mistaking what the man meant and with a last look at the shed he started for the gate, paused, darted back to pick up the bone. The man roared with laughter as Banjo dashed out into the street with his prize.

"You're a cheeky bugger, I'll give you that. Go on, you can have it."

Banjo ran off down the hill to the park and the woman said reproachfully, "You should have had a look at his ear."

The man closed the gate. "I've seen that dog knocking about a lot lately, he must live somewhere handy and that might teach whoever owns him not to let him roam about on his own."

"Poor thing," said the woman as she hurried inside out of the cold.

The falling snow was now denser, almost blotting out the golf course on the hill across the lake and naturally, the park was deserted, but that was all right with Banjo. His wound was stinging with the cold but that same cold helped to congeal the blood and the thick streak of blood-soaked hair on his neck and face was stiffening. The main thing was that he had a bone, plenty of time and a place out of the snow in which to eat it.

(158)

He went to the round wooden building where he had once spent the night, sprawled in the middle of the floor and commenced gnawing. The bone was very thick, hard and smooth, so polished he couldn't splinter off anything to eat but it was immensely satisfying to grind his teeth on it.

He took his time enjoying the bone, time enough for the wind to drop, the snow to stop falling and the cold to start the mercury plummeting.

Maybe due to the delayed reaction of the fight, the state of shock however mild which must accompany every wound, he dropped off to sleep with the bone between his front paws. When he woke, the temperature was still falling, hardening the ground and skinning the edges of the lake with thin ice. It was getting dark, time to feed, time to go back to town.

He felt the stiffening bruises when he had his shake, his shoulder hurt where Teddy had crashed him into the wall and when he swallowed, it was as though savage teeth were still clinging to his throat. As he trotted through the deepening dusk, the regular movement eased his shoulder and it was certain a sore throat wouldn't stop him consuming his dinner.

The streets in the shopping centre were as busy, or even busier, than when he had escaped from them that morning. Laden people were filling the boots of cars, queueing for buses, struggling into or out of crowded stores. The market was the same, everywhere hoards of people, people, people, and Banjo slunk on his way close to the walls. He wouldn't feed here, he would go to the seclusion of one of his cafés backed onto a quiet alley where he could be selective.

The plate scrapings were right royal. Roast turkey, pork, potatoes, sausages all nicely mixed with a heavy, dark coloured pudding and custard. He was eating earlier than had become his habit but he didn't feel quite himself, his coat was not keeping out the cold as it should and from time to time he shivered. But he ate his fill. Unconsciously he ate to comfort himself

He stood in the darkness of the alley shivering, for once not eager to be out and about, seeing and doing. That evening he wanted the warmth of a fire, the softness of a a rug, the companionship of a friend. And Mrs. Mountain's old house with its roaring fire had been so briefly his home that it never entered his head.

He came out of the alley and walked down the wide street with all the shops and as he was passing one of them, a very big store, draughts of warm air hit him as the multiple doors of the entrance constantly swung in and out. Warmth.

The lines of people pushing in and out of the doors were never ending, bulkily dressed in deference to the weather, and laden with bags and packets. Banjo wouldn't normally have tried to go into that turmoil, but he wanted warmth more than he had ever wanted anything so he nipped between two pairs of legs, through the narrowing gap of a spring-controlled door. A thin woman with a pinched, spiteful face tried to move back to avoid contact with his blood-caked neck.

"Look at that! A bloody filthy dog in the place!"

She meant the first adjective as a profanity, but it was apt, and the people pressing round the counters could not get out of the way. He just moved into any space that conveniently opened, once trying one too narrow, and he scraped his bitten ear on the hard edge of a shopping bag. The blood started to trickle again and more than one person, intent on inspecting the displayed goods, might well have wondered how blood had got onto the hem of a coat or knee of trousers.

Banjo wanted a quiet place in which to lie down, to let the warm air soothe the chilled ache from his bones, somewhere he could close his eyes. He found a little corner where a bannister curved at the foot of a staircase; he slumped on his belly, put his head on his paws and no one seemed to take any notice of him. It was noisy in the store but as his ague got worse the voices and tramping feet blended into a muted hum far away above him.

"Oy ... oy ... wake up!"

The voice came down in to the depth of his sleep, a commanding but not unkind voice. The store was quiet now with only the staff clearing up prior to going home. The man, the floor manager, standing over him was elderly and he was showing no signs of aggression. He was smiling.

(160)

Banjo had warmed through, he was comfortable and he didn't want to move. He turned his eyes up without moving his head. The smiling man persisted.

"Yes, I mean you. Time to go home."

The manager saw the blood when Banjo raised his head and the raw tenderness of the raggedly torn ear. He knelt down beside Banjo and ran his hand over the rough back.

"Now then. You're in a bit of a state, aren't you." He raised his voice, "Betty, fetch us some water and a clean rag, love. We've got a wounded soldier here."

Banjo could not have landed in kinder, more well-meaning hands, but of course he didn't know that. The manager had two dogs of his own and had taken the trouble to find out about dogs, how to keep and care for them. He could see Banjo had not been cared for lately and marked him correctly as a stray. In the time it took the girl to bring the water, he tried to make friends, stroking, talking, but a few minutes is little time in which to instil confidence in a sick dog. He soaked the cloth, stroking Banjo's back all the time and slowly held it to the wound. At the stinging contact Banjo changed from a passive invalid to a threatening enemy, hackles up, lips drawn and emitting the rolling growl of warning.

The girl, Betty, moved nervously back. "Leave it alone, Mr. Hanson. It'll go for you."

Mr. Hanson had already moved back, too well versed in the unpredictability of unknown animals to take any risks, risks an experienced vet would not take without proper equipment.

"Pity, but if he won't let me help him ..." He shrugged his shoulders. "Look the R.S.P.C.A. number up, love, and tell them. Tell them he's not mad or anything, just hurt, looks as though he's lost a fair amount of blood and I think he's got a fever. They won't be pleased on Christmas Eve, I don't suppose, but we can't help that."

The girl went away to telephone for aid for Banjo as the staff started collecting at the door, ready to go home. Mr. Hanson was responsible for seeing them out, checking the security and finally locking up, and he reluctantly left Banjo to attend to his duties. But Banjo got wearily to his feet and followed him at a dragging slouch, as though it was an effort to place one leg in front of the other.

As he neared the waiting people Banjo stopped, head held low, watching with disinterest as though he couldn't care who was going where.

The staff were all slightly tipsy, forgivably as it was Christmas Eve, from lunchtime drinks and there was a lot of well wishing and good-will kissing, as they filed out through the single door held open by Mr. Hanson.

"Merry Christmas, Dolly, give us a kiss."

"Don't do owt I wouldn't do!"

"Don't do owt I *would* do!"

"See you at the Mecca later, Janet."

"Not if I see you first."

They were laughing, happy at the thought of the holiday, the parties, the good times, and as two of them stood in the doorway saying their cheerios, Banjo moved. He did not move excessively quickly or furtively, he just got a sudden longing for a drink and decided to go to his tap at the bottom of the market. And Mr. Hanson had no chance of stopping him; he was out in the cold street and on his way before the manager noticed he had gone even though he brushed his trousers in passing.

The cold was worse, it bit into his bones, particularly his thighs and ribs and he was shaking again, shivering and trembling long before he got to the tap for his drink. And he didn't get his drink. Instead of the steady drip there was a long pointed icicle hanging from the outlet. He licked at the icicle, baffled. He crunched away the icicle and got a tremendous shiver, right through his frame, at the freezing contact with his mouth.

The snow had stopped again. The cold gripped silently, invisibly, but a slight ruffle of a breeze made a liar of the thermometer and temperature readings, the stirring of the air took away body heat and made the four degrees below freezing point unrealistic.

Banjo stood by his tap, hot-cold, shaking, quivering with a high fever, and in dejected misery he went to look for a warm place to sleep. Any place warmer than the outdoors would do, any place at all.

Chapter 9

(9)

Most of the shoppers had gone home. But from inside some of the still lighted shops came a lot of laughing and singing as workmates held their Christmas 'fuddles' before going home to the festivities proper. They came out in small groups, mostly; talkative, loud, happy at the prospect of long mornings in bed to recover from the parties.

Even Banjo could sense joviality which always meant friendship, and friendship meant kindness. So he stood on the cold pavement waiting for someone with whom he could make friends. He waited outside one of the brightly shining shops listening to the singing, the loud telling of crude jokes he couldn't understand, the possibility of companionship raising his drooping spirits a little.

The swing doors opened again violently, with such force that one of them jammed on an irregularity of the old stone step and a man came out at great speed—propelled by two other men. His hair was profuse and awry, his clothes dirty and work-stained and he skidded on the pavement, nearly falling. He turned to shout at the two men—large, grim men—an incoherent babble of which Banjo could not understand a word.

One of the men in the doorway said flatly,"Think on, Jackson, you're scratched. Go cause trouble somewhere else."

The man on the pavement continued to stand and shout but the two men took no more notice, turning and going through a second pair of swing doors. And they forgot to close the outside pair. The small draught of warm air they released enveloped Banjo in a brief moment of luxury before it was snatched away by the night: warm air tainted with smoke and the odour of packed bodies, promising heat to ease his aching bones and take the nip of frost from his ear. The stinging pain was changing to a deep throb and the light bruises on his body that he would normally have barely noticed were separate roots of nagging pain.

Timidly he passed through the open external door and pushed at the internal one with his nose. It moved freely on easy hinges and the smoke and noise swirled out again.

He was looking into the crowded bar of a noisy pub that was jam-packed with high-spirited people. Men and women were leaning against the bar but there was a clear passage from their feet to the wall, leading away from the cold of the street and Banjo didn't wonder or care where it led to. He gave the door another push, slipped through as it was swinging shut, and ran up the side of the wall. The revellers didn't notice him and he had no thought for anything but to get as far away from the cold street as quickly as possible.

At the end of the wall was an open doorway and from the room inside came a flow of even warmer air. This was where Banjo wanted to be. He went in without reconnoitring. Here the people were all sitting at tables, close-packed in the grey cloud of smoke, eating from plates and bags, drinking, but the food did not attract him. What did attract him were the stirrings of warm air, caused by the movement of feet and legs of the people sitting on the long upholstered seat attached to the wall. Close to the door the seat ended and it was easy to squeeze under the open end between the single leg and the support fixed to the wall.

The source of warm air was coming from two pipes fastened to the bottom of the wall, and drifting up against the lie of his coat in invisible wonderful waves. He lay down in the semi-darkness close to the pipes, giving an ecstatic, shivering yawn as the heat wrapped around him and started taking the aches from his bones.

The noise in that room might not have been there, the

singing, laughing, the occasional splinter of a breaking glass, the rattle of metal trays all combined into a receding hum when the warmth-induced sleep closed his eyes.

It was not someone's foot that woke him this time, it was furious barking, the angry, frustrated barking of a big dog. It drove through his tired mind, the barking and the shouting of a man. He wanted it to go away, to let him go back to sleep, but there was no let up.

"Come on, yer can't stop in 'ere. Out!"

The big dog, a lion-sized Alsatian, was crouched down looking under the seat at him. It was stopped from coming to the attack by a short, thick choker-chain. The publican had been doing his final check of the premises when his dog had scented Banjo, almost pulling him off his feet with a dive amongst the chairs and tables, his great head and shoulders scattering the furniture.

"*Come on!*" The publican was getting angry at being kept from the party going on up in the living quarters. "Yer'll wish y' '*ad* gone if I let Major at yer."

The tone of the voice told Banjo he was not welcome and the imminent threat of savagery by the Alsatian told him it was time to make tracks. The three-hour sleep had done him good, he felt more like himself as he came fully awake. He slipped out from under the bench, passed within inches of the huge snapping jaws and ran down the passage, pushed through the easy-moving swing doors and out into the freezing street. Behind he heard the bolts go home, the key turn in the lock and again he stood on the pavement in the cold night with nowhere to go. It seemed there was no place for Banjo.

It was quiet now outside; the only moving things were people looking for taxis and the taxis themselves, as they tore about ignoring the speed limits on this night of Bonanza. But there was no Bonanza for Banjo. Without thought or reason he set off north, possibly because that was the direction of his favourite playground, the park with two lakes, not that he felt like playing.

Once out of the city centre there were more signs of life, many houses still brightly lit and groups of people going from one house to another. Noisy people, shouting, laughing, singing. One unsteady man he passed stopped and bowed to him.

"A merry Christmas, dog," and his wife who was some way behind with friends snorted, "Silly sod! He goes barmy on whisky."

Banjo plodded on, knowing nothing of the peculiar ways people have of making fun.

All the way up the long road he kept passing merry makers on their way from party to party, all intensely determined to have a good time, none with any time for Banjo, until at last he came to the final group of shops with the clock tower in the centre of the road and beyond that the street where he had received his mauling from Teddy.

It may be that the greatest difference between human and canine psyche is imagination; humans have it, dogs do not. A lengthy campaign of attacks by Teddy would have eventually taught Banjo the inadvisability of using that street, but there had been only the one encounter, and at that moment the Bull Terrier was not tearing off his ear nor strangling him. Banjo felt no fear. Dogs are very material and concerned with the present, little else.

Because of the lateness of the hour there were no dogs to bark and be barked at—until he got to Teddy's house. That house and the one next door had lights on in every window and Banjo could hear the thumping of feet, the clamour of loud music. He was going on his aimless way down to the park when Teddy, who had been let out for a run and was anxious for another easy victory, barked his challenge. Banjo recognised the bark, his hackles went up and he faced his foe through the woodwork of the gate, matching snap for snap.

He wasn't afraid. The sting of his ear had died to nothing more than an inconvenient nag when he jerked his head, a handicap beneath consideration to one with no imagination and a very high pain threshold—and he was not aware he was one half ear short. The soreness of his throat, too, was not nearly bad enough to stop him answering the challenge, to symbolically acclaim that he was a male dog and the equal of any other. In a fair fight he was no match for the Staffordshire Bull Terrier, a situation in which a human would have either bowed the knee or resorted to trickery, but Banjo's lack of guile ruled out the trickery and his inability to resist a challenge ruled out running away.

However, the trickery was provided for him by the space separating the lower bars of the gate as against the size of Teddy. Great-hearted fighter though he was, Teddy was not quick on the uptake and the number of times he tried to squeeze through those bars to get at other dogs ought to have taught him the feat was impossible. But it had not.

When he tired of the barking ritual, he changed the tone of his voice to a rumbling, snarling growl and tried to drive his head out through the fabricated gate. He was stopped, as always, by the breadth of his skull at his ears, but, his lip-curled muzzle was showing on Banjo's side. That was enough for Banjo. He darted in and bit hard, midway between Teddy's nose and eyes. If Teddy had not tried to pull back Banjo would have followed his normal technique of trying to deliver as many bites to as many parts of Teddy's anatomy as possible. Naturally Teddy *did* try to pull away back through the bars and Banjo was not having that. He bit harder, clinging grimly to his struggling, barking enemy, bracing his feet and hauling back, giving vent with a few exultant growls of his own.

Teddy had never known defeat before, it was always he who handed out the punishment, he who made the other dog run away or back off and now he would gladly have been a party to a disengagement had that been possible. For once in his aggressive life, the other dog had the advantage and Banjo was hanging on as though he had no intention of losing it.

Tremendously strong though he was, Teddy, with his head confined by the bars, his chest pressed close up, could not get sufficient leverage and he was firmly caught in a trap of his own making, the cause of his own downfall.

Banjo's teeth had driven through his upper jaw bursting the fresh stitches. The blood started to flow and the taste of his own blood—he did not know it was his own— drove Teddy berserk. His barks and growls changed to a

(169)

high-pitched screech of pain, rage, frustration. He couldn't pull back, he couldn't go forward so he took the only alternative and tried to shake Banjo loose by moving his head up and down, thrusting up on his short, bowed legs and dropping his chin to the bottom rail of the gate. Up down, up down, a rough corner of the bars rubbing away the hair and skin from the side of his head.

Banjo didn't know why he hung on so grimly, certainly not from the fear of a freed Teddy coming over the wall at him for he was feeling no fear and he hadn't the ability to work that out in any case. But hang on he did, tenaciously, as implacably as Teddy had to his throat.

The guests in the house were making plenty of noise accompanying the record player but Teddy's howls of mounting pain cut through it enough for his master to hear—the true dog owner always seems to have one ear cocked for his pet.

He came running out into the drive with two curious friends trailing him.

"What's up, then," he shouted when he saw Teddy's forepart going up and down like a piston. Then he made out the shape of Banjo and bawled, "Leave him, leave him!"

His friends were with him when he leant over the gate to swipe at Banjo and that irked him more than anything else. Only half an hour earlier he had enjoyed going into every detail of Teddy's latest victory over the shaggy grey dog and now they were here to witness Teddy getting the worst of it—and *he* would never hear the last of *that*.

The dogs were blocking the gate and when Teddy's master unlatched the gate and heaved, not only did he have Banjo's weight to pull but the bottom of the gate was jamming on Teddy's paws, preventing it from swinging and increasing the unfortunate dog's cries of anguish.

"*Back*! Back, you bloody thing!" he yelled at Banjo and only then did the fact that he was offending a human penetrate Banjo's mind. So intent had he been on clinging to Teddy nothing else had registered. When he did realise, he hesitated a moment before releasing his captive and it took another angry shout to make him open his jaws.

(170)

When Teddy plucked his head free, he first shook the blood from his streaming lip onto the trousers of the guests—who were not amused—and then hobbled away on his bruised feet still whimpering, his appetite for fighting fully sated for that night.

In the next garden the lady who had shown some sympathy for Banjo in the first fight had come out again followed by some of her guests. They were all tipsy, including the hostess who shouted across the hedge.

"Set him onto another dog once too often, didn't you? That'll be a few more quid in vet's fees."

"I didn't set him onto him," protested Teddy's master truthfully. "It's that walking rag-bag out there that's caused all the trouble." Switching from the truth to inaccurate guesswork.

Out on the pavement, Banjo cocked his head as if listening intelligently, almost cheekily, and Teddy's master, who was also the worse for drink, picked up a clod of soil and hurled it with all his strength but poor aim high over Banjo's head.

Forgetting there were ladies present he yelled, "Piss off!"

The two neighbours had never been the best of friends and the seasonal amount of whisky helped to magnify what was normally a cold indifference into active dislike.

The woman, watched by her interested guests who were now crowding in the doorway, shouted, "Don't use that language in front of me, you ... you ..."

"Go on, Fran, say it," encouraged a jovial voice from the doorway. "We'll close our ears."

Teddy's master remembered his injured pet and, with a black scowl across the hedge, hurried indoors where everyone was trying to keep their party clothes clear of Teddy's dripping blood. He would insist on shaking his head.

"Hmm," snorted Fran in a that's-put-paid-to-him way, and the unpredictable alcohol fumes fuzzing her brain suddenly changed her from a crusader into a Florence Nightingale.

"That poor dog out there's been running around injured all day. Let's have a look at him."

(171)

Fran and guests all trooped out into the street to where Banjo had decided to sit down to listen to the exchanges. A little of the ache had come back into his bones, not with the previous intensity but enough to make his forelegs tremble slightly now the excitement and physical activity was over.

"Look at the poor thing," said Fran sadly.

"Yes," agreed one of her guests, "even a dog shouldn't be out on a night like this. And it *is* Christmas."

"Let's take him in and feed him," suggested another, an idea that found all-round approval.

Fran was no dog lover, but nor was she a dog hater and she had nothing against giving this one a night's shelter.

"All right, let's see if he'll come. Come on, boy, come inside out of the cold."

The words were just sounds to Banjo, but what was very material was the smell on the hand of the man who came close to beckon him to follow. They smelled of food. There was food where those hands had come from and it was highly likely there would be food wherever they were going. Banjo went with them for all the world like an obedient, very well trained animal.

"Understands every word y'say," slurred one man admiringly.

When they had crowded back into the house, into the bright light, Fran who was fairly houseproud had the stirrings of misgivings when she saw the dirty, tangled mass of Banjo's coat at close range. But she was essentially kindly and came to a compromise.

"Come on, in the kitchen, you won't hurt the tiles in there."

As she spoke, she clicked her fingers under Banjo's nose, filling his nostrils again with the scent of rich foods and he trotted beside her along the corridor and into the kitchen.

"Bloody hell, that's the most intelligent dog I've ever seen," one man said, shaking his head and following Fran.

"You go into the party," he told her, "I'll see to the dog."

It was a very large house, old and stout with spacious rooms and high ceilings and the kitchen was a sight for any dog's sore eyes. The middle of the floor was taken up with a huge wooden table and every inch of the table top was taken up with plates, trays and dishes of food of every kind which threw off a mouth-watering cocktail of a scent; turkey, pork pies, chipolatas, tarts and cakes. Every kind of thing the omnivorous Banjo delighted in eating.

But it was Christmas and Banjo's attendant, who knew nothing about dogs, treated him as he would a human— the whisky he had consumed had a lot to do with it. The first hospitable move was to offer a drink. He found a deep pie dish in a cupboard, opened a bottle of pale ale and gurgled it into the dish under Banjo's nose.

"My uncle's old dog used to like this."

Banjo had been getting enough water for survival, enough to prevent him from being really thirsty, but not since he left Mrs. Mountain's had he had a proper deep drink. He looked at the frothy liquid, caught the smell, took one tentative lap and stood back.

"Go on," urged the man, "it'll do you good."

Banjo stood with his head down looking with longing at the liquid he couldn't drink.

"All right, then, maybe you like milk."

The beer went down the drain and a bottle of milk came from the refrigerator. Banjo showed him he had hit the mark this time, his furious tongue scooping the dish clean and then he chased the dish across the floor to wipe every drop from the corners.

The man laughed. "Steady on, there's plenty more."

He poured out a second half pint and when Banjo put that away, a third from another bottle. When that was gone Banjo transferred his attention to food, looking up at the laden table.

He was given a chicken leg and a piece of pork pie, Christmas cake and mince pies, in fact a little of almost everything from that bountiful table and it all went the same way, vanishing with two or three quick gulps. The man laughed at his voracity, unaware that a dog is more than likely to eat to bursting point, until it overloads the stomach to such an extent that that stomach rebels and rejects the whole lot. Banjo had been used to controlled

(173)

amounts of food except for the last weeks when the scraps on which he had been living contained nothing like the richness of this meal. He would have gone on eating for as long as the man wanted to drop food in the dish but the man wearied of the novelty and wanted to get back into the party. He poured out the last of the second bottle of milk and patted Banjo on the head.

"Behave yourself," he said and went out leaving Banjo shut in the kitchen.

With a truly full belly and sated thirst, Banjo made a desultory inspection of the kitchen, yawned and stretched mightily, curled up under the table and slept the sleep of the just.

He was disturbed by murmuring voices. Apart from the voices, the house was quiet with the guests all gone.

Fran and her husband were standing in the doorway, whispering.

"What should we do?"

"Just leave him, he'll be all right."

"Do you think we'll be able to get rid of him? I wish I hadn't brought him in now."

"Ye-es, he'll go straight home when we let him out later."

"I hope so."

"Stop worrying and come to bed. We can't turn him out at this hour."

"No. All right."

The kitchen light went out and they tiptoed unsteadily away.

Banjo had not moved, he had watched through eyes barely open, lids slitted to stop the bright light from making the giddy nausea worse. He sighed loudly through his nose when the light went out, but still the waves of dizziness washed over him to make his head spin. He didn't want to move but the floor was moving beneath him, swooping and rolling, making his stomach heave and lurch. It had been a day of extremes. His body had been subjected to pain-induced shock, the breath-taking cold outside and the muggy heat of the department store and the pub; he had known the triumph of victory and the joy

(174)

of unlimited food and drink; a combination of events which would test the stoutest of constitutions. And when his body started to object to the treatment it had received with a series of convulsions his unfailing instinct told him what to do. He got to his feet and tottered, head down, towards the back door.

He was trying to get outside, but the door was firmly shut. His body arched, his stomach jerked and he vomited a heap of undigested food at the foot of the door. He retched again and again as his stomach pumped itself clear, until he stood exhausted, head hanging, but with an immense feeling of relief instead of that swirling sickness. Slowly he returned to his place under the table and went to sleep.

The second time his sleep was disturbed by noises overhead, someone moving about in the bedrooms. It was daylight, enough of the winter sunshine coming in through the curtains to see by.

Banjo felt himself again now, more or less, a bit sore at the throat and ear but nothing to worry about. He did, however, have something else to worry about, the growing, pressing, urgent need of a tree or lamp-post. The quart of milk wanted to join the food in the open air and his swollen bladder was creating havoc. He whimpered and ran to the back door which was still closed. The only other possible way was out of the kitchen to look for some other means of exit; the habit engrained into him at the Holmeses of never soiling the inside of the house was still strong in his make-up. The vomiting he had been unable to prevent, but to relieve himself indoors was unthinkable.

Banjo pushed through the swing door which led out of the kitchen. Across the hall was the lounge, a long, L-shaped, thickly carpeted, expensively furnished room. He raced around but nowhere could he find an opening into the garden. It didn't occur to him that one bark would have brought someone running downstairs to let him out, all he could do was trot around the room in desperation until the demand of nature became overpowering and he had no choice but to disgrace himself.

That was when he noticed the lounge was like no other

he had seen. It had a tree. A tree! A strange tree bedecked with small lights and various trinkets, but a real tree—he could smell it—with tiny spikey leaves some of which had fallen onto the carpet. He ran under the low bottom branches to sniff at the trunk and find if any other dogs had used it lately. No other dogs had and, furthermore, the trunk didn't sprout out of the ground as trunks should but out of a barrel of hard-packed earth. Around the bottom of the barrel were scattered packages of different sizes, so many he could not help but walk on them. This was not as things should be. The base of the trunk should have been ripe with the perfume of other dogs; ideally it should be growing from thick grass and should not be surrounded with parcels. But it was a tree and therefore fair game. He made one more circuit of the barrel before choosing his spot—always a ritual of vital importance—and then raised his leg.

He stayed on three legs a long time and anyone who knew him would have said he was grinning.

Twenty minutes later Fran, her husband and three children did not have reason to grin. The children were teenagers who had been allowed a little wine at the party and had slept late like their parents, and the whole family came down in a herd for the present-opening, the youngsters laughing and dragging their parents who were bearing up bravely, all things considered.

The youngest was a plump, merry girl who, not believing that age should precede beauty, was first on her knees to reach under the tree to where she had previously made the location of her presents.

"Yee-ack!" she shrilled, springing back to her feet, "I'm soaking."

There was a dark patch of damp on each of the knees of her pyjamas. Fran bent to look suspiciously under the lower branches and she moved back, wrinkling her nose.

"Phew!" She glared at her sons. "Have you two been having one of your so-called jokes, 'cos if you have ..."

The boys protested indignantly that they would never joke where such important things as presents were concerned, so the man of the house bent down to investigate

(176)

further. Gingerly he lifted parcels with finger and thumb, tossing them out into the open. The ball point inscriptions on the first three had run and blurred and were nearly illegible.

"The whole bloody lot's wet through and the carpet's like a puddle. What on earth is leaking?"

He looked for tell-tale water marks on the ceiling and walls and frowned at his wife.

"I don't understa—"

"*That bloody dog*," she bawled, "*It's that bloody dog.*"

"Oh, my lovely jeans," her daughter moaned, eyeing a soggy parcel.

The youngest son touched with his toe the damp bundle addressed to him. "Jeans? What about my Six-Million-Dollar-Man suit?"

"And my—"

"Where's that bloody dog?" said the man of the house with all the threatening menace striven for by actors in thriller plays.

That 'bloody dog' was where he had returned after relieving himself, back under the kitchen table, but at the sound of voices he had snapped awake, hopeful of more refreshments. He came through the kitchen door gaily wagging his tail, grinning his 'good morning' at these people who had befriended him and to whom he would find it easy to attach himself. He was met by five furious people, who, for some reason unknown to him, had undergone a complete reversal of attitude. He stopped two yards from the doorway, hesitant, uncertain of what he had done wrong but knowing by the manner of these people that they were displeased with him.

In the same kind of situation at the Holmeses, he used to retreat into his kennel and skulk there until things had died down, so now he quickly went back to the place he deemed had been appointed to him under the kitchen table.

They crowded into the kitchen, all shouting angrily—but shut up at once as though a master switch had been thrown. The children had been allowed to over-eat at the

(177)

party by their parents as a sort of appeasement for the overdrinking they themselves had fully intended doing, so there were five stomachs still overfull with various combinations of alcohol, pop, rich and sickly foods and these five stomachs queasily turned and churned in harmony at the unappetising sight of the rejected contents of Banjo's stomach. Moaning, groaning and wailing, they turned in a body and hurried from the kitchen.

"Who," asked a distraught Fran, "is going to clean that up?"

"Who," asked her husband accusingly, "let the bloody thing in the first place?"

Their brood chorused, "Not me."

"Not me, either," said Fran's husband very definitely. "I'm off back upstairs to get shaved."

His children didn't shave but they went with him just the same.

Fran stood in the lounge amongst the debris of the party, dirty plates and glasses everywhere, the carpet sprinkled with fragments of nut shells, crumbs, sweet wrappings. Scattered around the lovingly decorated Christmas tree were the soaking parcels, under the tree the pool that would somehow have to be cleaned up and in the kitchen that pile of ... Her hungover mind refused to consider the revolting prospect any more at that moment.

The air in the room was stale with tobacco smoke and alcohol fumes and was not doing her any good at all. What she needed was some good deep breaths of fresh air and a cup of tea ... to make the tea she would have to go into the kitchen. She put the thought of tea to one side for the moment and opened the windows wide. She stood on the top step with the snap of Christmas Day frost tingling her cheeks, pinching her nostrils. She shivered in her nightdress and dressing gown but revelled in the clean freshness of the morning, and shuddered at the thought of the chores that must follow. She gritted her teeth on remembering her stupidity in bringing the dog inside.

The flow of clean air drifted through to Banjo. Currents of air came from openings. Openings led to the outside. Banjo wanted to be outside now the household was angry with him. He came from under the table, put his face up and followed the airflow to the front door.

The woman was standing in the centre of the doorway but there was plenty of room for him to slip through out into the bright invigorating morning. The gate stopped him. Fran's privet hedge was too high and wide for him to jump and the gate was a high wrought iron affair which a horse could not have leapt. He turned back to look his mute question at her.

Even the few breaths up to then had done her good, helped to clear her head and perk up her spirits and she had a twinge of conscience for the shaggy, dirty, uncared-for dog with the sore-looking half ear. Perhaps he was not entirely to blame for his crimes. Cyril, the man who had fed Banjo, had told them about the prodigious amount of food the dog had put away—poor thing was probably half starved most of the time—and after drinking a quart of milk anyone would have been ready to have an accident.

She hugged her dressing gown to her sides, ran down the path and opened the gate.

"Go on," she said in a low voice that held a touch of contrition, "you won't be the only one who's been sick this morning but, God, dog, *I've* to clean it up."

Banjo liked that tone of voice, it held no threat and was therefore the voice of a friend. He didn't go out, he didn't move, just stood looking up at her and she pulled the gate wider, making a pushing movement with her right hand.

"I said go on. Whoever owns you will be wondering where you are."

Banjo went, but there was no spring in his step and he walked instead of trotting. He went along the road, down to the park without looking back. Fran closed her gate, ran back to the warmth of the house and the cleaning-up operation. When she shuddered it was not from the cold.

It was another deserted morning in the park with only Banjo, the sparrows and a few old crows to prove the world was not dead. Automatically he went on one of his circuits, the one round the lake. He would have liked some company, canine or human, to socialise with but there was

(179)

no one, nothing in that wintertime wilderness within the boundaries of the big city.

Animal minds, like human minds, are conditioned by events. His earliest memories were of the Holmes family who gave him love and care, channelled his mind into accepting the firm belief that he belonged to them and would never belong to anyone else—or perhaps that they belonged to him. When circumstances had forced them to give him away Banjo could not have been expected to understand what was happening and why. With the only home he remembered so fresh in his mind, with his yearning for Paul so strong, he had not been able to accept Mrs. Mountain as his family, kind as she had been. Given time he would have done, but he didn't live with her long enough for even the tiniest of roots to start growing. He had failed to find Paul, the only person he wanted, and had enjoyed the spell of being virtually a wild dog, but character and nature is immovably deep-seated and now Banjo knew another longing.

Aeons ago, somewhere on this planet a wild dog, the first, must have crept up to the shelter and warmth of a fire-lit cave to give himself up to Man so that he and all his descendants could be subjected to the will of Man until those descendants had wiped from memory and instinct the urge to run free. Always gregarious with the desire to run in packs, they included Man amongst their numbers, happy to live with him, in some cases work for him, do his bidding until, in the modern world, they became fully dependent for their existence on the human race. Amongst the necessities in life for a dog is a master and a permanent place of abode whether that be a mansion, a hovel or the roving caravan of a gipsy; it is all the same to a dog as long as he has a familiar place. Banjo had no place. In that cold, silent park in the season of goodwill he wanted one as much as he had wanted anything.

Chapter 10

(10)

That day and the one after were very, very lean. The rubbish bins behind his café contained almost nothing edible and he had to visit them all to get what amounted to less than half a meal. Twice he made nervous approaches to the hot-dog stand, both times dodging a missile thrown with a torrent of abuse, and after that he gave up knowing that tantalising smell of cooking food held no hope for him.

The market was closed, barring him from his second and only other food supply. He suffered the same gnawing in his belly that had driven his ancestor into the domination of the cavemen and on the second afternoon, Boxing Day, hunger drove him to the cave freshest in his memory; the home of Fran.

The high, iron gate was closed but through the curlicues and bars he could see lights in the windows, people moving about. Not aware that he had spoiled several Christmas presents or given Fran a sickening task on the one morning of the year when it would be least appreciated, he looked for a way through the privet hedge. He found it close to the boundary with Teddy's garden, a small gap in the thick stems close to the ground. It took an effort, flat on his belly, to wriggle through but that afternoon he would have tried to get through the eye of a needle for something to eat.

The front door was closed so he went round the house to the back and the back door was closed too. He could hear movement inside the kitchen and smell the beautiful smells from the food on the table. With his mouth filling with saliva he put his nose to the bottom of the door to sniff and sniff and sniff.

Banjo had no imagination but he did have a memory to project mind-pictures of brown meat, golden pies and other favourite foods which worked in association with the scents coming under the door to make him whimper beseechingly. To and fro along the bottom of the door he went, drooling and softly whining to signal his hunger.

As though he had shouted 'Open Sesame' at the mouth of Aladdin's cave the door opened, letting out a gust of warm air that swamped his nostrils with the maddening aromas. He made as if to dive inside but stopped dead when he saw the girl Amanda, who shouted in some alarm:

"Ma-am, it's that dog again!" as though Banjo was a fugitive robber or rapist, and she partly closed the door again to keep him out. Fran's head appeared in the opening over her daughter's shoulder.

"Go away! Go on, go away."

Together woman and girl verbally tried to drive him off but it is doubtful if their voices registered. Keen hunger is a sharp spur and Banjo's limited brain was filled with visions of things to eat, the things he knew were in that kitchen. In that universal canine way Banjo had fastened his eyes on Fran's—he instinctively knew she was the superior—to stare in an unblinking plea through his fringe.

They stayed there for several seconds, the females looking out, Banjo looking in. He tried to hurry things up with a pitiful whine. For all his ugliness, his filthy unkempt condition, he couldn't have adopted a pose more calculated to play on the hearts of two females.

Amanda said, "I think he's starving."

Fran said, "*I* think he's lost."

With a spark of excitement, Amanda said, "Shall we feed him?"

"He's filthy—and look at the mess he made. What's your father going to say?"

"We can feed him in the yard."

Banjo listened with rising hope to the voice tones that were no longer unfriendly, keeping his unwavering gaze on the woman when the girl went away. She was not away

(184)

long, coming back with a handful of dark turkey meat that no one wanted. She tossed them out through the gap one piece at a time and was treated to an exhibition of catching that wouldn't have discredited the sharpest slip fielders. She threw six finger-sized shreds and not one hit the ground, Banjo leaping and turning acrobatically in that surprising way that belied his stubby body and ungainly legs. And each piece was swallowed whole with ravenous desperation almost before his feet touched the ground again.

Amanda giggled. "Isn't he good. I'll get him some more."

She got him some more and they went through the performance again.

"I'll get him some mo—"

"No," interrupted her mother, "*I'll* get him some more. If we're going to feed him, we're going to feed him properly."

She came back with the same deep pie dish Banjo had been fed from before. It was heaped with tasty scraps of turkey, pork and crackling, pie crust. She noticed that hungry as the dog obviously was, he waited until she had set it on the ground and stepped back before he attacked it. Attacked is the only word for the way he devoured that food, his first real meal in two days.

"Look, he's got a disc on his collar, it might say where he lives," the girl said.

"Wait till he's finished eating."

Banjo chased the last particles around the dish and sat back; now it should be drinking time. He could have eaten more, much more had he been given the run of that kitchen, but he was no longer tormented by the stomach pains and he was content to await further offers.

Fran went up to him cautiously, twisted his collar to bring the disc to the side of his neck, parted the long hair of his grimy coat and rubbed the dirt from the tag.

She laughed. "Guess what they call him?"

"Scruffy?"

"Banjo!"

"Banjo? Banjo? I've never heard a dog called that before."

(185)

"Well, it suits him if you look at the marking on his back."

When he heard his name Banjo grinned, his sides pumping in and out with happy panting. Fran read the reverse side of the tag.

"I told you he was lost. He lives right over on York Road. He belongs to someone called Paul Holmes, and you," she wagged her finger at Banjo, "will have spoiled his Christmas by running away."

Banjo was getting what he wanted, attention; his sides pumped faster making his breathing sound like an old steam engine.

The girl said slowly, "He's mucky, but I think he's a nice dog, really, if you don't count what he did on Christmas Eve. What are we going to do with him?"

"Your father and John won't be back till about six, we'll wait till they come and take him home. We'll put him in the garage. You go in and shut the front doors."

"It'll be cold for him in there ..."

"Well he's not coming into the house in that state. I must have been mad to let him in on Christmas Eve. He might have fleas."

"Aw ..." Amanda was feigning petulance but her mother intended to be firm.

"Never mind aw, he's staying in the garage. Come on, it's getting cold."

The girl went through the rear door of the garage and as Fran led the unresisting Banjo in by the collar he heard the main door squealing closed. They left Banjo alone with a final word for him to behave himself, the closing of the rear door cutting off the entreaties of the girl who was still arguing about something.

What was cold for Fran was certainly not cold for Banjo. The light had thoughtfully been left on for him and when he had made a tour of the workbench, the oil drums, the walls and doors, he settled down for a nap. He didn't get it.

The girl came back staggering under the weight of a steaming bucket. She put it down close to Banjo, went out again and returned with another.

"Now," she said, businesslike, "we're going to get you

(186)

clean or Dad won't even let you in the back of the car. Stand up."

Banjo stayed where he was, knowing what buckets of water meant and not liking it. She dipped into the soapy bucket and brought out a dripping cloth.

"Come on," she repeated sternly, "stand up!"

He turned his head away, apparently suddenly interested in a blank wall and under the pretext that what he could not see did not exist. But the girl did exist, so did the cloth soaked in warm soapy water and it landed with a slap in the middle of his back. Banjo whined sorrowfully, hating bathnight but knowing from sad experience that there could be no escape. There never had been, never would be, but that didn't mean he would endorse the hated process by co-operating. He didn't attempt to run away—there was nowhere to run—but he did walk slowly about, making things difficult as Amanda rubbed and scrubbed energetically. First a good lathering all over with the suds and then the steaming rinse during which he found it necessary to have a periodic shake and douse the girl with a cloud of flying droplets.

"Keep still, stop it," she shouted, words that had not the least effect. She ended his bath with the supreme insult of tipping on him what was left of the rinsing water and when he shook himself that time, he got his own back by drenching her.

She spluttered, blinking the water from her eyes, "If you were *my* dog, I'd—" she laughed at his woebegone drooping stance. "You do look funny all wet and fluffy—and if I don't get changed, I'll catch me death. Wait here." A superfluous order in the light of the fact that she firmly closed the door behind her.

It took another three good shakes to rid his coat of the excess moisture. The shakes, starting at his head and shoulders, rippled down his body to the tip of his extended tail and when he started to dry out he began to look fairly respectable, allowing for his unclassic lines. His white marks were now white again and the light grey distinguishable from the dark. The shaking had dropped his coat

(187)

into the correct lie and his fringe was more like a curtain of woollen strands than a tangle of filthy string.

The girl brought Fran back with her. "Look, isn't he nice now?"

"Not bad."

"He's lovely!"

"We-ell," Fran smiled, "you can hardly say that, but he's passable."

"Can he come in, then, so he won't get cold?"

Fran sighed, promising herself that she *would* stop giving in to her only daughter, but nodded, "But only in the kitchen, mind. If you let him in the lounge, I'll just throw him out."

Amanda took his collar. "Come on, Banjo, but you've got to be good."

He didn't have to be good for very long before father and son came home loudly extolling the footballing skill of Leeds United, a flow of enthusiasm which dried up when they saw who was lying on the centre of the kitchen floor.

"What?" started Fran's husband with lowering brows, but his daughter knew he was even easier to handle than her mother and she led him by the hand to where she had arrayed an attractive plate of sandwiches in front of the fire.

"I'll tell you while you're having your tea, Daddy. Sit down, you must be cold. And don't *you* eat them all," she ordered her brother who had needed no invitation to spoil the pattern decorated with cress and lettuce. Fran, knowing her daughter and her husband, found something to do in the kitchen. She was better out of it.

Banjo lay on the tiled floor and panted away happily. He had been fed, given a drink of milk, he was warm and nearly dry, what else could he want? He did want something else before the girl came back. He went to stand at the door. Fran was washing dishes with her back to him so he whined.

"What do you want?" He whined again. "Oh, that's what you want, is it? Well you're on your own, if you take off again it's your own fault."

She let him out into the dark, saw him disappear into

the back garden and left the door ajar for him. He wasn't away long, and came back to lie in the same place.

Fran raised her eyebrows. "Looks as though it might have been our fault on Christmas Eve. You seem to know about the simple things."

Amanda came from the lounge grinning. Her mother asked, "Well?"

"Dad say's he'll take him. I knew he would. We're taking you home, Banjo."

Banjo grinned and wagged his tail.

It was Amanda who took him outside, leading him by the collar, round to where the estate car was parked at the front, and persuaded him to jump into the rear section. She sat in the back seat to keep him in place and to make sure he didn't jump over.

Her father had a rough idea of the location of the street inscribed on Banjo's identification tag and he found it without difficulty.

"There's someone in, anyway," he said as he climbed out. "You stay with the dog, Amanda, while I go see them."

The girl saw him outlined against the lighted window, saw the door open, the short conversation, the door close, and he was back. He explained as they drove away and the girl put her hand over the back of the seat to stroke Banjo's head.

"Poor thing. They must have been rotten, Dad, just to abandon him like that … he's a nice dog, isn't he?"

Her father grunted noncommittally, sensing the first silken threads of the net his daughter was weaving to trap him.

Banjo was quite happy in the back of the car, unconsciously drawing in the strings he had attached to the girl's heart that afternoon when he had jumped to catch the meat and when he had let her, even if with bad grace, bath him.

"And you haven't got fleas, have you?" Amanda asked him, stroking away. Banjo grinned and panted, her father rolled his eyes to heaven.

Banjo was the main topic that evening, the subject of much family political manoeuvring, the girl lobbying her mother and brother John to her cause and her father being backed by the oldest boy, Howard. At that early stage only

(189)

Amanda and John really wanted to keep Banjo, the floating vote of her mother given mainly to keep the peace, and only her father was actually against the proposition. Howard sided with him in the furtherance of his desire to own a certain second-hand motor cycle which he knew was going cheap.

Although a three to two vote is by any standards a clear working majority, the main dissenter was not entirely of the opinion that households should be run as republics, more as a patriarchy subscribing to the divine right of fathers. So Banjo's future hung in the balance for some time. Amanda's remark that her father's arguments were codswallop in view of the recent implementation of the Sex Discrimination Act brought cheers from her benches but gained little ground in the debate, but what finally won the battle—and will undoubtedly continue to win the battles in spite of the official levelling of the sexes—were her tears when Howard callously declared the only place for stray dogs was the Dogs' Home. Howard actually didn't care whether Banjo stayed or not as long as he would be able to refer to the way in which he had stood by his father in a time of need when he introduced the subject of the motor cycle.

The man of the house begrudgingly gave in to the apple of his eye, but not without administering a stern lecture that Banjo would be regarded as her property and her responsibility, the onus of his welfare falling on her shoulders.

It was exactly the same kind of speech Madge Holmes had given to Paul, and in the same way Banjo entered his new family as he had done the Holmeses, growing on them steadily and inexorably, claiming them for his own and making them take him into their hearts.

First it was laid down that he should live in the garage, that on no account would he be allowed to roam the house—a state of affairs that Amanda put up with for one day. It was barbaric, she said, to make such a nice well-mannered animal live out in the cold. So his dwelling place was elevated to the kitchen provided he never took one step through the doorway into the lounge.

Nobody was quite sure how Banjo wangled it but inside a month he was getting away with taking the freedom of the bedrooms as well as the lounge, running up and treating the groaning family to a reveille of barks when he thought they had overslept.

Every day he went the short walk down the road to the park with two lakes, always on the lead with Amanda or John, to run or swim off his boundless energy. He loved swimming, never tiring of paddling in hopeless pursuit of the ducks who simply took to the air if he got too close.

Amanda, his official owner, had one concern. Her friends at school spoke lovingly of their Poodles, St. Bernards, Great Danes, and other such noble breeds while she could only refer to Banjo as Banjo. It was on one occasion when he was swimming after the ducks that gave her the idea. She urged him from the water (he had not forgotten the recall), clipped on the lead and raced home, bursting in on her father who was engrossed with his football pools.

"Dad!"

"What?"

"Where do dogs come from? I mean, how did all the breeds start?"

Knowing it was useless to go on forecasting the probable results of Saturday's matches until he had satisfied her in some measure, he put down his pen.

"From the wolves," he said, hoping that would be enough. It was not.

"They can't have done."

"I've read," he expanded, trying to keep in mind that Charlie George would be fit for Saturday, "that all dogs came from the wolves, thousands of years ago, and that it's man's messing about with the breeding that's produced all the varieties. I'm not sure, but that's what I've read."

In this case his word was good enough for Amanda.

"So you mean that once there weren't any Spaniels or Alsatians?"

"Something like that."

"And that some man crossed two kinds of dog and said they were a breed?"

(191)

"That's all I can think of."

"So," she mused, "anyone can start a new breed, then."

"It's not as simple as *that*, there's the Kennel Club and
..." He was talking to himself; she had raced up to her
room with Banjo to do some deep thinking.

On the Saturday afternoon when the fans of the house had
trekked off to Elland Road in the hope of watching
Manchester United receive a trouncing, Amanda set off
with a brushed and spruced-up Banjo, along a nearby
avenue where three of her schoolfriends lived, dog-owning
schoolfriends. As she had hoped, one of them saw her from
a window, waved for her to wait and came out to show off
her Golden Retriever.

"Isn't he lovely," crooned the classmate.

"Yes," Amanda had to agree, "two of my cousins have
got Retrievers."

The classmate looked curiously at Banjo, who was
grinning through the gate at the Retriever, saw his odd
colouring, spherical head, clothes prop legs and shaggy
coat, and there was a sneer in her voice when she asked:
"What's that?"

Amanda's smile was superior, a smile that suited the
founder of a breed. "Oh," she replied with a calculating
casualness, "he's a rare one. Only one of his kind in the
country."

With the smirk fading, the classmate pressed, "But what
is he?"

With the timing of an actress, Amanda paused before
announcing, "He's a Yorkshire Duckhound. Come on,
Banjo."

Banjo grinned again at the common or garden Retriever
and bounced away with his mistress, full of the sheer joy of
living, of belonging, of having a place of his own.